Harlequin
th...

**Harlequin Romance is going to shower you with...
diamond proposals and dazzling weddings,
sparkling brides and gorgeous grooms!**

The Australian's Society Bride
by Margaret Way

Her Valentine Blind Date
by Raye Morgan

The Royal Marriage Arrangement
by Rebecca Winters

Two Little Miracles
by Caroline Anderson

Manhattan Boss, Diamond Proposal
by Trish Wylie

The Bridesmaid and the Billionaire
by Shirley Jump

Whether it's the stunning solitaire ring
that he's offering, the beautiful white dress she's wearing
or the loving vows between them, these stories
will bring a touch of sparkle to your life....

Dear Reader,

Harlequin is having a diamond anniversary—and we're all part of it!

Diamonds are a girl's best friend. Marilyn Monroe taught us that little gem many years ago, and some believe it's true to this day. Not romance readers, though. We put our trust in relationships. The old man-woman thing. The eyes meeting across a crowded room. The quickening pulse as you catch sight of that gorgeous guy in your doorway. The soft, exciting crush of his lips on yours. The swell of his hard biceps under your fingers…whoops—where was I?

Oh yes—diamonds.

We may not rely on diamonds as the life support Marilyn was singing about, but they are special. We love them for their beauty and for what they represent—commitment, eternal love and faithfulness. Funny thing—these are all elements of our fascination with romance fiction of the Harlequin variety.

So enjoy the 60th anniversary. Read a lot of romance novels—and here's hoping there are more diamonds in your future.

Celebrate!

Raye Morgan

RAYE MORGAN

Her Valentine Blind Date

DIAMOND
BRIDES

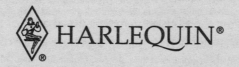

HARLEQUIN®

TORONTO • NEW YORK • LONDON
AMSTERDAM • PARIS • SYDNEY • HAMBURG
STOCKHOLM • ATHENS • TOKYO • MILAN • MADRID
PRAGUE • WARSAW • BUDAPEST • AUCKLAND

Recycling programs
for this product may
not exist in your area.

ISBN-13: 978-0-373-17566-6
ISBN-10:   0-373-17566-3

HER VALENTINE BLIND DATE

First North American Publication 2009.

www.eHarlequin.com

Printed in U.S.A.

Raye Morgan is a fool for romance. With four grown sons, love, or at least heavy-duty friendship, is constantly in the air. Two sons have recently married—that leaves two more to go, and lots of romantic turmoil to feed the idea machine. Raye has published more than seventy romance novels and claims to have many more waiting in the wings. Though she's lived in Holland, Guam and Washington, D.C., she currently makes her home in Southern California with her husband and the occasional son. When not writing, she can be found feverishly working on family genealogy and scrapbooking. So many pictures—so little time!

**Share your dream wedding proposal
and you could win a stunning diamond necklace!**

**For more information
visit www.DiamondBridesProposal.com.**

CHAPTER ONE

BAD timing.

Max Angeli shoved the single red rose he was carrying into his pocket as he flipped open his mobile and barked a greeting, resigned to the certainty that whatever he was about to be told was going to create a new level of chaos in his life. First problem—the dance club he'd just walked into was too noisy. Lights swirled and the heavy drumbeat of sensual rhythms pounded. The brittle clink of crystal liquor glasses vied with high-pitched feminine laughter to fill the air with a sort of desperate frivolity. He already despised the place.

"Hold on, Tito," he said into the phone. "Let me get to a spot where I can hear you."

He could tell it was his assistant on the other end of the call, but he couldn't understand a word he was saying. A quick scan of the crowded lounge located the powder room and he headed for it. The sound level improved only marginally, but enough to let him hear what Tito was saying.

"We found her."

Max felt as though he'd touched a live electric wire. Everything in him was shocked. Closing his eyes, he tried to take it in. They'd been searching for weeks, with no apparent leads, until this last tip that his brother's ex-girlfriend, Sheila Bern, might have traveled by bus to Dallas.

His brother, Gino, had died just months before. Sheila hadn't surfaced at the time, but she'd contacted Max months later to say she'd had Gino's baby. When he'd asked for proof that the baby was indeed his brother's, she'd vanished again. He'd almost given up hope. And now, to hear that she'd been found…

"You found her?" he repeated hoarsely. "Are you sure?"

"Well, yes and no."

His grip hardened on the mobile. "Damn it, Tito…"

"Just get over here, Max. You'll see what I mean." He rattled off an address.

Max closed his eyes again and memorized the information. "Okay," he said. "Sit tight. I've got to get out of this blind date thing I got myself involved in. I'll be right there."

"Okay. Hey, boss? Hurry."

Max nodded. "You got it." He snapped the phone shut and turned back to the noisy room, tempted to head straight for his car and forget the woman who was waiting for him somewhere in all this annoying crush of revelers. But even he couldn't be quite that rude. Besides, his mother would make him pay. She might be sitting in a terraced penthouse in Venice at the moment, but she had ways of reaching across the ocean to Dallas and turning on the guilt machine. Even though she was American, he was the Italian son, and he'd been raised to value keeping his mother happy.

Hesitating on the threshold, he scanned the room and searched for a woman holding a red rose—the match to the poor, straggly item he'd belatedly retrieved from his suit pocket. All he needed to do was find her and let her know something had come up. Simple. It should only take a minute.

Cari Christensen bit her lip and wished she could drown her red rose in the glass of wine that sat untouched in front of her.

"Five more minutes," she promised herself. "And then, if he's not here, I'm going to drop that rose into a trash basket and melt into the crowd. Without that, he'll never know who I am."

He was almost half an hour late. One half hour. That ought to be good enough. She'd promised her best friend, Mara, that she would go through with this, but she hadn't promised to spend all night at it. She sighed, carefully avoiding eye contact with any of the interested males shouldering their way past the bar, wishing with all her heart that she was home snuggled up with a good book. Mara meant well, but couldn't understand that Cari wasn't looking for Mr. Right. She wasn't looking for mister anyone at all. She didn't want a man. She didn't want a relationship. She didn't even want a husband. She'd done that once already and it had turned her life into a living hell.

"Once bitten, twice shy," was her motto. She had no intention of going through that sort of heartbreak again.

But how could Mara understand that? She'd married her childhood sweetheart, settled down in a cute little ranch house and had two adorable kids. Her life was full of piano recitals and pictures on the refrigerator and picnics and kittens. Cari's marriage hadn't turned out that way. They were two very different people, despite the fact that they had been best friends forever.

"Some people find the golden ring swimming in their cereal in the morning, slip it on their finger, and go skipping through life," was how Cari tried to explain it to Mara. "And others drop it in the sand at the beach and spend the rest of their life digging to get it back."

"That's just silly," Mara had retorted. "Do you think my life is perfect or something?"

"Yes, Mara, I do. Compared to mine, it is."

"Oh, Cari." Mara had taken her hand and held it tightly. "What happened with Brian and…and the baby…well, it was just horrible. It shouldn't have happened to anyone, much less someone like you who deserves so much better." She blinked rapidly as tears filled her dark eyes. "But you've got to try again. There's someone out there for you. I just know it. And once you find the right man…"

The right man. Was there such a creature? Even Mara didn't know the details of what her marriage had really been like. If she did, she might not be so quick to try to throw her back into the deep end of the pool.

"Mara, will you please give it up? I'm perfectly satisfied with my life the way it is now."

"Oh, Cari!" She sighed tragically. "I can't bear the thought of you sitting at home sniffing over old movies on one more Valentine's Day."

Was that what this was all about?

"Wait! Hold it. I don't give a darn about Valentine's Day. It's a made-up holiday. Who cares?"

"Don't try to fool me, Cari Christensen. I know you better than that."

"Mara, no!"

"You need a man."

Mara looked so fierce, Cari had to laugh. "I don't know why I let you be my friend."

"Because you know I'm looking out for what's best for you."

Cari sighed. She knew she was beat. But she had to pretend to fight on. "I don't need anyone looking out for me."

"You do, too. I'm your assigned fairy godmother. Get used to it."

"No."

Mara, of course, wouldn't give up at all, and that was why Cari was sitting here in the Longhorn Lounge, holding a sad little red rose and waiting for a man named Randy who Mara had assured her was the exact match for her.

"Just wait. He's special. You'll be surprised."

So she was doing this for her friend. She planned to smile a lot and act interested in Randy's tales of male world conquests, eat a nice dinner in the dining room here at the lounge, get a headache about time for ordering dessert, make a nice apology and head for home. From then on, her answering machine could take care of things for her. And maybe Mara would give up. After all, she'd tried.

The door opened and a man entered, opening his cell phone as he came. Tall and dark and dressed in a beautifully cut suit instead of the jeans and casual shirts most of the men here wore, he grabbed the attention of a lot of onlookers. Something about the way he held himself drew the eye. Or it might just have been the fact that he was the most ruggedly handsome man she'd ever seen this side of the cinema. His thick, dark hair was exquisitely cut and yet managed to give the impression of being a bit long and a bit careless—as though it had just been ruffled by a renegade breeze or a lover's fingers. His broad shoulders strained the silk suit as he turned, and the knife-sharp crease in his slacks only served to emphasize the muscularity of his thighs. A Greek statue brought to life and disguised in a modern business suit.

She shivered, and then had to smile to herself. One thing was certain, this couldn't possibly be her man Randy. And she was glad of that. In her experience, high-powered, incredibly handsome men were the worst kind. But she had to admit he had his attractions.

Eye candy, they called it. Lucky she was on a diet.

She pulled her attention away and looked at her gold watch. One more minute and she would be free.

"Sorry, Mara," she would say on the phone to her friend tomorrow. "He didn't show. Consider it a sign. And don't think you're going to get me to do this again."

A shadow fell over her and she looked up to find a rather beefy-looking man in a Stetson and tight jeans grinning down at her.

"Hey, little lady, why don't you let me buy you one of them fancy drinks with the umbrellas and fruit and such?" he suggested, all swagger and no appeal.

Inwardly she groaned, but she had enough control not to let it show. "No, thank you, cowboy," she said, trying to remain pleasant as she slid down off the bar stool and turned toward the door. "I was just leaving."

"No need to rush off," he said, effectively blocking her exit route. "Why, you're as pretty as a cactus flower, ain't ya'?"

She flashed him a tight smile and lifted her chin, letting him know she was no pushover. "And just as prickly, honey. Better stand back. You don't want to get stuck."

His face darkened. "Now you listen here…"

But just as suddenly as the cowboy had appeared in her line of sight, he now faded away, because someone bigger and more impressive had come into the picture, and everything else seemed to melt around them. She felt his presence before she saw him and she pulled in a quick breath, almost a gasp. Slowly, she raised her eyes.

Sure enough, it was the man she'd seen coming in the doorway a few minutes before—the man she'd been so sure could not have anything to do with her or her life. He was standing before her, holding out a bedraggled red rose, and asking her a question. Her mind seemed to go blank. She swayed. And she couldn't hear a word he was saying.

"What?" she asked numbly, looking up at him as though she were blinking into the sun.

Max was caught between interest and annoyance. He wanted to get this over with and get out of here, but he'd already bungled things. He'd managed fairly easily to find this pretty lady with the head full of blond curls and a frilly little black dress. Her attire revealed a figure that was full and rounded in all the right places and legs that made looking worthwhile.

But the problem was, he couldn't remember her name. His mother had said it often enough, over and over, whenever she told the old story of how the Triple M Ranch had been swindled from her family. This was the daughter of the woman who had done his mother dirty—but what was her name again? Something-something Kerry, wasn't it?

"Miss Kerry?" he repeated when she didn't hear him the first time.

"Oh!" she said, looking shell-shocked. "You can't be— I mean— Are…are you…?"

"Exactly." He waved the rose at her and nodded toward the one she held. "I was hoping we would have some time to get to know each other tonight," he said smoothly. "However, sadly, it is not to be. Sorry to do this to you, but something has just come up and I'm going to have to take a rain check."

"Oh."

He stopped, nonplussed. She seemed rather sweet and she was definitely embarrassed. Not what he was expecting. Was she taking this as a sort of rejection? Well, he supposed that made sense from her point of view. But instead of the arrogant siren he'd imagined from the tales his mother told, a woman whose ego probably had too hard a shell to be bruised in any way, she took this personally. Did she think he'd taken one look and decided she wasn't worth wasting time on? Despite everything, he didn't want to hurt the woman.

"My mother sends her best wishes," he said, his gaze flickering appreciatively over her pretty face. Interestingly, she wasn't his usual type. He tended to favor fashion models—long, cool ladies who were decorative and yet mature enough to know the score. Young innocents wanted to fall in love all the time. That sort of clingy attachment was neither in his nature nor in the cards. He'd spent a lifetime observing the human condition. In his opinion, falling in love was for suckers who were in denial and hoping for a fairy tale. He considered himself too hard-nosed to fall for such nonsense.

But there was something appealing about this young woman just the same. She looked intelligent and quick, even though she was gaping a bit. Her eyes were a brilliant shade of blue, framed by thick, dark lashes and accented by a pert nose that seemed to have a dusting of freckles just for spice. Her hair, the color of spring sunshine, was a stylishly tangled mass that kept falling over her eyes, making her reach up to push a way through in order to see him clearly.

Hardly what he'd expected. From what his mother had told him, he'd been sure he was going to dislike her intensely. Now he wasn't so certain.

"I'm hoping we'll be able to do this another time," he said, actually meaning it. "May I call you tomorrow?"

"Oh," she said again, her lovely crystal eyes enormous as she stared at him. "I…I guess so."

Her vocabulary wasn't extensive. Or maybe he'd been a bit too brusque. His friends and employees had accused him of that more than once, and he regretted it. He didn't mean to be rude.

But he had no time for this. Shrugging, he gave her a cool smile and turned for the exit. He was almost out the door when he remembered the stupid rose in his hand. She might as well have it. After all, what was he going to do with it?

Turning back, he found her still watching him, wide-eyed. Something about the look in those huge blue eyes…

"Oh, what the hell," he said impetuously. Leaving her behind would be like telling a puppy you didn't want him to follow you home. "Why don't you come along? We'll stop and grab something to eat somewhere else."

He congratulated himself right away. It was a good

idea. Yes, that way he had the original obligation out of the way and yet didn't do any damage to the hope of a future relationship. At the same time, he wouldn't feel quite so guilty when he called his mother later. Brilliant!

"I…well, maybe…" Cari cleared her throat.

She wasn't sure why she couldn't seem to get a full sentence out. This wasn't like her. But the fact that the man was so diametrically different from what she'd pictured had completely thrown her for a loop and she was taking some time to get over her shock. For the moment, she seemed to be putty in his hands, and the next thing she knew, she was hurrying out of the club with one of those same hands planted squarely between her shoulder blades. She was going with him, or so it seemed. She glanced back, not sure of the wisdom of heading into the dark of night with a stranger.

But he was Mara's husband's cousin. At least, that was what her friend had claimed.

The funny thing was, as she looked back at the noisy club, she thought she'd caught a flashing glimpse of a red rose being carried by a tall, sandy-haired young man with glasses. But everything was happening so quickly, she hardly registered that sight. And her companion tended to fill up her attention. So she went along with him, half skipping in her wobbly high heels to keep up, as they hurried to his long, low and very flashy car.

"Oh, my gosh," she said as he opened the door to the passenger's seat for her.

"It's a Ferrari," he said, frowning slightly. "Surely

you've seen Ferraris around town. I thought Dallas was crawling with them."

She nodded as she sank into the luxurious leather. "Of course. I've just never been in one before," she told him, then winced. Maybe she should have kept that to herself.

He lowered himself into the driver's seat and leaned forward to punch the address they were aiming at into the GPS, then turned to look at her with one slick eyebrow raised. "From what I've heard of your background, I would have thought fast cars and living in luxury were right down your alley."

She frowned at him, puzzled. Did he have her mixed up with some other blind date? "Who would have told you a thing like that?"

He gazed at her for a moment, then shrugged, looking reasonably adorable in his faux bewilderment. "Texas," he muttered, starting the car. "This place always surprises me."

And that statement surprised *her*. She was about to mention that Mara had said he'd grown up outside of Galveston, but her power of speech got lost as she noticed again just how incredibly good-looking this man was. Everything about him screamed wealth and power. His suit had probably cost more than her secondhand car. His gorgeous black hair, his wonderful tanned skin, the way his thighs swelled against the fabric of his slacks, all created a picture guaranteed to set off the female heart rate. His shirt was open at the neck, revealing more tanned skin and just a hint of crispy, crinkly chest hair. If she were the swooning type, she'd be out cold by now.

But she wasn't, she reminded herself sharply. Not her style at all. And there was another thing. All this embarrassment of hunky male riches didn't add up somehow. Mara's husband was basically a cutie, but to think that he had someone like this in his family boggled the mind.

But it was too late to say anything, anyway, because the low, slinky sports car had taken off like a rocket. As her body slammed back against the soft leather seat, she felt as though she had to hold on for dear life, her heart in her throat.

The car came to a stop at a light. She gulped in a mouthful of air and turned sharply toward him, letting him know she hadn't loved it.

"Wow. Do you always drive like this?" she asked a bit testily, pushing her hair back with one hand. "If so, you must have a permanent seat named after you at traffic court."

He seemed surprised by her strong voice and point of view, but laughed.

"I'm just trying this baby out. I picked her up at the showroom earlier today and I wanted to see what she can handle." He grimaced. "But I don't know the streets around here very well, so I think that will do it. Sorry. I should have warned you."

He gave her a lopsided grin, feeling no chagrin at all over the pleasure that surge of power had given him. But his grin faded as he looked at her.

That crazy, curly hair kept falling down over her eye and he had the oddest impulse to reach out and brush it back for her. The thought made his fingers tingle. He found himself looking at where her tiny, shell-like ear was peeking out from among the curls, and then staring at the smooth, creamy skin of her neck and imagining his lips there and his tongue…

The car behind them honked and he realized the light had turned green. He turned his attention back to his driving. But his mind was on the woman next to him in the car. Something about her tickled his fancy in a strange and unfamiliar way.

And suddenly her name came back to him. Celinia Jade Kerry. How could he have forgotten a name like that? Celinia Jade. Rather a mouthful, wasn't it?

"Mind if I call you C.J.?" he asked her a bit sardonically.

She blinked, truly puzzled. "Why would you do that?"

"For short. It's easier to remember."

She frowned, her nose wrinkling. "But…"

He turned the car onto the freeway and they were off again. Her words disappeared in the roar of the engine, and he had to merge with a tangle of speeding traffic, which didn't leave him time to ask her to repeat them.

Funny, but now that he thought about it, his mother had told him Celinia Jade Kerry would fit right in with the type of woman he usually dated—the sort his mother, Paula Angeli, actually tended to roll her eyes at.

Not that she knew C.J. very well, but she did know the woman's mother. Or had, years ago.

"Betty Jean Martin was her name before she married Neal Kerry, the man who stole my family's ranch," his mother had told him over morning cappuccino just days ago. They'd been sitting on the terrace of her Italian home, overlooking the Venice canals. "She was my best friend, but when she married Neal behind my back, she became my worst enemy."

He'd nodded, having heard the story so often, it was a family legend. He had a sneaking suspicion that his mother had thought *she* was going to marry the man— before her friend Betty Jean had whisked him to the altar—and that in that way she would have been able to get her ranch back. All things considered, he couldn't be too sorry that hadn't happened at the time. Besides, his mother had met his father, Carlo Angeli, shortly after, and her life had changed for the better, at least monetarily. That often happened when one married a millionaire.

Still, Max knew the marriage hadn't been a happy one. His father had rarely been around, and his affairs with the wives of his best friends were legendary. His mother's life had been wrapped up in her two sons— and in bittersweet memories of a childhood on the Triple M Ranch outside of Dallas, Texas.

"I'm sure Celinia Jade will be just what you're used to," his mother went on, waving the letter that had come from the daughter of her old friend. "I still keep in touch with enough old Texans to know what's going on. She's a clotheshorse with nothing on her mind deeper than the latest hemlines and whether her newest shade of lip gloss makes her mouth more kissable. Sound familiar?"

"Have you been listening in on my phone conversations again?" he'd teased her.

And that was when she'd rolled her eyes.

"Don't you get it, Mama?" he told her with loving humor. "I don't date women for their conversation."

"Then you'll probably get along perfectly with the young Miss Kerry." Paula had frowned, looking at the letter again. "It's odd to hear from her after all these years. And to have her ask to come visit us."

"And just lucky timing that I'm leaving for Dallas in a few days and can check out the situation." He looked at her, noting the dark circles under her eyes. She'd been looking more frail lately. Ever since Gino had died. It broke his heart to see her this way.

"What do you suppose she wants?" he'd asked casually, though he was pretty sure he knew.

"Money." His mother sighed, shaking her head of graying curls. "The word is she's in deep financial trouble. Her parents are both gone now and she's spent her way through what little they left her. She's looking at you as one big old ATM machine, I have no doubt."

"Interesting," he'd murmured, a plan developing in his head. "You're sure she still has the Triple M Ranch?"

"Oh, yes. She'll never give that up. Who would?" She winced and he knew she was remembering that her own family had done exactly that—something she could never forgive. "But she probably needs funds to keep it running."

"A loan?"

Paula laughed. "Hardly. She'd never be able to pay it back. My guess?" She smiled at her son. "She asks a lot of questions about you in her letter. I think she'll try to get you to marry her."

"Many have tried," he noted dryly, only half joking.

"But no one has come close yet," she agreed with a sigh.

He'd grunted noncommittally, thinking it over. "Call her," he suggested. "Put her off about her coming here, but tell her I'll be in town and would like to meet her. Set up a rendezvous."

She nodded reluctantly. "What are you planning?" she asked.

He smiled at her. "Mama, you know property acquisition is my specialty. I plan to talk her into selling us that ranch you loved so much."

Her eyes sparkled for just a moment, but she shook her head. "She'll never do it."

He shrugged. "We'll see."

"Oh, Max, do be careful. Don't let her charm you. If she's anything like her mother was…"

He'd dropped a kiss on the top of her head as he started for the door. "I'll give her that old famous Texas sweet talkin' you taught me all about when I was a whippersnapper. She'll be begging to turn the ranch over to us in no time."

Looking back at her as he reached the door, he could see a sad, faraway look in her eyes and knew she was thinking about Gino, his older brother who had died a few months before. That look on her face brought a catch to his throat. He would do anything to bring the joy back for her. Anything.

And that was the mission that had brought him to Dallas.

CHAPTER TWO

"So, TELL me, C.J.," Max said, looking sideways at Cari as they exited the freeway and turned into a dark, spooky-looking industrial area. A quick flash of lightning lit up the horizon, then disappeared as quickly as it came. The air was electric with possibilities. "How's life out on the ranch these days?"

She eyed him and shook her head. His conversation was becoming more incomprehensible to her. Her little house could be called ranch-style, but she certainly wasn't running any cattle in the yard.

"What ranch?"

The ranch your family stole from mine, he thought cynically, his mouth twisting. Are you going to pretend that never happened?

But aloud he said, "The ranch you live on, of course."

She shook her head. What in the world had Mara told this man in order to get him to spend an evening with her? She knew her friend was subject to occasional flights of imagination, gilding the lily, so to speak, but this was ridiculous.

"I don't live on a ranch," she told him firmly. He might as well know the truth.

"Ah. I suppose you're just a normal, everyday Texas girl." His voice belied his words. His sarcasm was showing.

But she nodded vigorously, becoming exasperated. "Yes, I am."

He chuckled. "What is it with you Texans? The popular myth is that you're all such big talkers, but all the Texans I meet are always trying to pretend they're just average folks, no matter how filthy rich they are or how much land they own."

She was at a loss. Surely Mara hadn't pretended she was from a wealthy family—a wealthy ranching family. Mara knew better.

"But we *are* mostly just average folks," she said defensively.

"Hah. *Se non è vero, è ben trovato.*"

The things he was saying were odd enough, but even odder was the fact that she was beginning to detect what sounded like a faint Italian accent, and that last outburst seemed to seal the deal.

"You know something?" she said accusingly. "You don't sound like a Texan."

"*Grazie,*" he replied with a casual shrug. "I'm only half-Texan, after all. I hope you can forgive my mistakes."

"Oh." Half-Texan! And the other half was evidently

Italian. How had Mara missed that tiny detail? She bit her lip, wondering if she'd offended him.

"So what did it mean, what you said a minute ago?"

He smiled at her. "I said it's a good story, even if it isn't true."

Before she could express fresh outrage, his phone chimed. He pulled it out of his pocket and looked at the screen.

"It's my mother," he said, sounding surprised as he pulled over to the side of the road. "She's calling from Venice." He flipped his mobile open.

"Your mother?" Cari gaped at him. She'd heard Italian men were attached to their mothers, but this was ridiculous.

"Sì, Mama."

He said something into the phone in what she assumed was Italian. It sounded like Italian. It even looked like Italian. Cari couldn't catch anything she recognized, but she watched the whole thing, fascinated. There was a lot of near-shouting and gesticulating, and suddenly he pulled the phone away from his ear and said, "Would you like to speak to my mother?"

She gazed at him in horror. His mother? Why on earth would she want to speak to his mother? What would she say?

"Not really," she said, shaking her head vehemently.

He said something else in Italian and clicked the phone shut. Turning, he eyed her narrowly.

"So the old resentments still live, do they?" he noted,

his gaze pinning her to the back of the seat with its dark, stormy intensity.

"What are you talking about?"

"The fact that you wouldn't speak to my mother."

Oh, this was just too rich. She'd signed on for a few hours of hopefully friendly conversation with a strange man, meal included, and that was about it. There had been no extended-family privileges implied in the deal. Now she was getting annoyed. Really annoyed.

"What am I supposed to talk to your mother about?" she asked heatedly, then waved a hand in the air. "I suppose I could give her a critique of how her son handles blind dates. But I'd hate to be insulting at this early stage of the evening."

He laughed, his gaze traveling over her face appreciatively. She glared at him.

"But listen," he said, his grin changing to a thoughtful frown. "I don't know what she's talking about. She says someone called and left a message that I was late to meet you." He shrugged, making a face and looking at her for confirmation. "I wasn't late. I was early."

She held his gaze. "You were late."

His frown deepened. "So you were already calling people and complaining that I wasn't there as early as you were?"

"I didn't call anyone." She couldn't have called anyone. She had a sudden picture of her phone, attached to the battery charger, still sitting on her kitchen counter where she'd left it. Darn. That made her feel naked and unprotected. A girl needed a good phone, especially when she was on a crazy and confusing blind date like this one.

"Well, somebody knew about it and called my mother."

Cari began to feel as though she were on a rapidly moving merry-go-round with oddly formed horses and scary faces leering at her out of the shadows. This entire date was becoming more and more surreal.

"Let me get this straight. Your mother's in Italy. Why does she care about whether you were on time to meet me or not?"

He gave her a slow smile and a long look, one that made her feel strangely languorous. Funny, despite how annoyed she was, she had to admit this was one sexy man. Given a chance, he could turn on the charm and wipe away most of her irritation.

"Because she's a caring person," he said smoothly. "And she wants us to get along well. For old-time's sake."

As she puzzled that over, his phone rang again. Max saw that it was Tito and barked, "Go," into the receiver.

"Where are you?"

"About a block away. I'll be there in a minute." He glanced at Cari. She seemed absorbed in the view outside her window. "Does Sheila know I'm coming?" he asked softly.

"Well, no."

"Why haven't you told her?"

"Well…"

"Have you filled her in on the parameters of the situation?"

"Actually, no."

"Why not?"

"Listen, boss, like I told you, she's not exactly here."

"But you said…"

"The baby's here."

That struck him like a thunderbolt. The whole point of this operation had been to find the baby. Gino's baby. Finding Sheila was secondary, but he hadn't expected them to be separated.

"I'm almost there," he said, signing off and dropping the mobile into the center bay. He turned to look at Cari. Why had he brought her along again? Hmm.

"Where are we going?" she asked, thinking maybe she should have established things like this before she'd agreed to go along with him.

"To take care of some…personal concerns." He put the car in gear. He'd thought he was going to be confronting his brother's ex-girlfriend, trying to get the truth out of her as to whether she'd had a baby with Gino. Now he knew she wasn't there. But a baby was. What did that mean? He was going to assume the baby was Gino's until someone proved different.

Turning to check for traffic, he pulled the car back into action.

"It should be right around this next corner. Ah, here it is."

"This is it?" Cari gazed at the run-down apartment building and frowned. Loud music was coming from an upper bank of windows. A dog was rummaging in a pile of papers near the entryway. One of the street-lights was broken, casting a pall on the area. She thought she saw someone withdrawing into the shadows across the street. This was not a neighborhood she would have ventured into if she'd been doing the driving.

"I thought we were going to get something to eat," she mentioned hopefully, thinking a nice bright restaurant on a busy street would be better than this gloomy place.

"We will." Leaning forward, he looked up at the ugly building and frowned. "I just have a little business to take care of here. I'll make it quick. Wait here."

No way. Cari looked at the empty street and shivered. "Actually, I think I'd rather go where you're going."

"Your choice." He shrugged. "Come along, then."

As he got out of the car and looked at the neighborhood, he couldn't really blame her. He didn't know Dallas well, but he was pretty sure nice neighborhoods didn't look like this. He couldn't leave her on her own out here, no matter how well he locked up his fancy car.

On the other hand, he didn't want her intimately involved in his family business. There was already too much family mixed into all this. Maybe it hadn't been such a brilliant move to bring her along after all.

He gazed at her speculatively as she came to join him, noting again how her riotous hair spun a magical frame around her appealing face. The ruffles of her bodice shimmered, giving her movements a fluid look, and her short, filmy black skirt followed suit with a flirty tantalizing style. There wasn't a hint of slick sophistication about her, just down-home, sexy woman. The sort of woman who made you think of crisp clean sheets on a big, wide bed. Was he allowed to think about her that way?

That made him laugh a little. What would his mother say?

Oh, Max, do be careful. Don't let her charm you. If she's anything like her mother was...

That was what she'd said, but he knew she didn't really think he would do anything hasty. Oh, she was serious about getting the Triple M Ranch back, but what she really wanted was for him to charm C.J., bewitch her, work on her emotions and manipulate her into selling it back to his family.

He'd been confident. From what he'd heard of her, he'd assumed this daughter of his mother's old rival would be just the sort of woman he was used to, beautiful and spoiled, born and bred to the flashy nightlife and the party scene where those with money tended to play. From what he'd seen so far, his read had been way off. Could he handle a woman like this? Was a little charm going to do the trick? Looking down into her clear, intelligent eyes, he had to admit this wasn't going to be as easy as it had seemed from across the Atlantic.

And what would happen if he let her follow him into the apartment he was planning to visit? The last thing in the world he wanted was a witness to his pending interview with whatever he would find there. A cool gust of a breeze chased leaves from between the buildings and brought the smell of pending rain. She shivered and he glanced up the driveway, noting where Tito had parked his white rental sedan.

"I've been thinking," he said, giving her his most winning smile. "Things aren't working out quite the way I'd thought they would. More complications have arisen than I expected. I'm going to have my assistant drive you back to the club. You can wait for me there. Tito will take good care of you."

She flashed him a look and raised her chin. "Forget it. I'm not switching partners at this late date."

His head went back as though she'd hit him. Was she implying…? That floored him. He came off as throwing his weight around sometimes, but he didn't like being taken for a jerk. "No, wait, you've got the wrong idea."

"Listen," she said frankly, tossing her hair. "I'm not accusing you of anything. But this has been one weird blind date so far. I like to keep my feet on the ground and my head out of the clouds. I think I'll just stick with you until you take me home."

"Ah. Better the devil you know, is that it?" He tried to act in his usual debonair fashion, but at the same time, he gazed at her uneasily. This was the woman he'd thought he was going to manipulate? Obviously, those plans were due for a rethink. But that would come later. Right now, he had other problems on his hands.

"This might not be pleasant," he warned her. "I'm not sure what we're facing here. So be prepared for anything."

She shrugged, wondering if he had noticed how her fingers were trembling. She was nowhere near as sure of herself as she tried to sound. When she'd said this date was weird, she'd been soft-pedaling the circumstances. She'd been bowled over at first by his presence, his confidence, his obvious savoir faire, and she'd been intimidated. But that was then.

Now, with the calls from the mother and the visits to slum neighborhoods, she had a bad feeling about this whole situation. He might be Mara's husband's cousin, but he was not your usual Texas boy. She'd have to keep this man in her sights and stay on her toes.

"If there's a problem, maybe I can help," she suggested. "I don't want to drag your assistant away when you need him most." She managed a stilted smile. "Don't worry, I won't get in the way. But I'll be in the background the whole time, ready to help if you need me. In the meantime, you won't even know I'm there."

His gaze was skeptical. "Right." He grimaced, but decided to play this one by ear. He ran a hand through his thick hair and sighed.

"Okay. If you're up for this, let's go on in and see what Tito has gotten me into now."

The building was dirty and smelled like day-old food. They found the apartment quickly enough. Max knocked and the door opened. A short, stocky man built like a fireplug greeted them nervously, nodding when Cari was introduced, his mind obviously on the business at hand and not on her.

"Let's see it," Max said, and Tito stood back to let them in.

Cari followed. She walked into the room totally unprepared for what she would find. The two men went quickly to the far end of the room, and at first she couldn't see where they were headed. When she caught sight of the baby crib, she froze.

No! Not a baby. Oh please, not a baby. Her breath caught and panic fluttered in her chest. Memories of her own four-month-old baby, Michelle, flooded her senses, hitting her unexpectedly. She wasn't prepared to deal with this. Cringing, she almost whimpered aloud.

It had been almost two years since the car accident that had taken the lives of her husband, Brian, and Michelle, their much-adored infant. Two years where she'd avoided every possibility of coming face-to-face with a real, live baby. She turned blindly, her impulse to rush out into the hallway and then away, as far away as she could get. Anything to escape the pain that seeing a baby like this represented.

Just as she hit the doorway, the baby began to cry. She stopped, unable to take another step. There were little gurgling sobs at first, then full-fledged piercing screams.

Turning, she looked back. A baby was crying. A baby needed comfort. Everything in her, every instinct, began to pull her back. Babies were tiny, helpless things with little waving arms and tiny kicking feet. They needed help. She was a woman, naturally equipped with the talent and emotions custom made for doing that. And yet...

She stood where she was, unable to take those steps that would bring her back to the baby's crib, unable to take steps out the door. Closing her eyes, she tried to catch her breath and still the wild beating of her heart. The look, the feel, the smell of her own lost baby filled her head. And the pain was almost too intense to bear.

Max's entire focus was on the baby. As he looked down at the dark-haired infant, his heart swelled with bittersweet anticipation. Was there a hint of Gino in that little face? Did the hands look like his brother's? Was this child all that was left of his brother's life? That was very possibly the situation. He would move heaven and earth to find out. And if it turned out to be the case, there was no way he would let this baby go.

"Boy or girl?" he asked the stalwart assistant standing beside him.

"Boy."

He supposed he should have known. The gown, the blanket, everything was blue. Despite the cluttered, messy condition of the room, things inside the crib looked clean enough.

"Name?"

"The babysitter says his name is Jamie."

"Babysitter?" For the first time since he'd come in the room, he raised his gaze from his study of the baby. "There's a babysitter?"

Tito nodded. "I told her to wait in the bedroom."

Max nodded back, then his eyes narrowed. "Where's Sheila?" he asked, naming his brother's girlfriend.

He'd only met her once. She was pretty, of course, and nice enough in her way, but her way tended to be a ditzy combination of brainless chatter and limitless desire for luxurious things. She and Gino were no longer an item when he was killed in the crash of a small plane. No one seemed to know what had happened to her. It was only months later that she began calling, claiming she'd had Gino's child, demanding money.

Tito's shrug was all encompassing. "The babysitter doesn't know. She says she was hired three days ago, and Sheila was supposed to be back in twenty-four hours. She has no contact number and Sheila hasn't called."

"Have you searched the place for phone numbers or addresses?"

"Of course. I haven't found anything relevant."

"Damn. Well, we can't just wait here."

"The babysitter said she was getting pretty scared herself. She was about on the point of calling the police when I got here."

"But she didn't?"

"No. At least, that's what she claims."

"Good." Max nodded again. "We'll get a local lawyer to handle this before we speak to the authorities."

Tito looked at him intently. "So you plan to take the baby?"

"Of course."

Tito nodded, but as if on cue, the baby began to fuss.

Max stared down at it. So did Tito. The fussing got more serious.

"It's crying," Tito said at last.

"Yes. So it seems." Max backed away a bit. Crying babies were not within his sphere of experience and he wasn't sure he wanted to know more.

Tito tried wiggling his fingers in front of the baby's face, but he only cried louder.

"It won't stop," he noted, beginning to look worried.

Max frowned, uneasy as well. "No." He looked at his assistant. "Was it crying before?"

Tito shook his head. "It's been asleep, I think. I know it wasn't making this kind of noise."

"It is now." Max winced as the decibel level increased.

"Well, what do you do when they cry?" Tito asked his boss, seemingly at a loss.

Max's frown grew fiercer. "How the hell should I know?"

The two men looked at each other, then back down at the baby. The mood was grim.

By now, Cari had managed to cross the room and was right behind them. She could just barely see the baby. He was crying as though his heart would break, holding nothing back. Her fear, her panic, was gone now. Her heart thumped in her chest, but she had things under a fair modicum of control. Taking a deep breath, she pushed her way between the men.

"Don't knock yourselves out looking for the off switch," she advised tartly. "They don't have one."

Max stepped back, seeming relieved as she reached the crib and curled her fingers around the bar. Steeling herself, she looked down, bracing for the sight. A mass of dark hair, fat cheeks red with crying, eyes squinted shut, two little fists waving in the air—this child looked nothing like hers. Relief flooded her and she closed her eyes for two seconds, then glanced down again and spoke to him.

"Hey little fellow," she crooned. "What's all this about? Don't you worry. You're going to be okay."

The sound of a feminine voice stopped the last cry in his throat and he opened his dark brown eyes and looked up at her. A remnant sob shook him, but he stared at her curiously as though she were something brand-new and possibly very interesting.

She smiled. He was adorable. Reaching down, she gathered him up and took him into her arms. And then she closed her eyes and let the feeling wash over her. She had a baby close against her. That special sort of enchantment had been her daily experience for such a short time before it was taken from her. And now, for the first time in two years, she could feel it again. Tears welled in her eyes.

"You can handle this, then?" the man who'd brought her here was saying.

She nodded without looking at him. She didn't want him to see that her eyes were wet.

Max stared at her. He wasn't always as sensitive as he should be to women's feelings, but he could tell something was going on here. He just wasn't quite sure what it was, and Tito beckoned from the door to the bedroom. He hesitated only a moment before he decided she was okay, and he turned and went into the side room to question the babysitter.

Cari held the baby gently and cooed, rocking the tiny body, until all whimpering quieted. The little eyes closed, long, dark lashes fluttering against rounded cheeks, and then he was still. She kissed his head and hummed softly. It seemed so natural. Her own baby had trained her well, though she didn't want to think about that. Blocking out the past was a part of accepting the present for her right now. She'd done a lot of time in her own personal agony and she couldn't live that way forever. But she'd spent much too long trying to avoid all contact with babies, hoping to avoid the pain memories brought with them. Now that she'd been thrust into this situation and forced to deal with it, she found she was in a special sort of heaven and she didn't even look up when the men came back into the room. She was floating on feelings and ignoring everything else.

When she heard the woman's voice she looked up in surprise, but hardly paid attention as the older lady left the room, Tito leaving close behind her. Vaguely, she was aware that this had been the babysitter and that Tito was driving the woman home, but it seemed to have nothing much to do with her enjoyment of this wonderful baby.

Max watched her for a moment, surprised to see how quickly she'd adapted to a style of nurturing he didn't remotely understand.

"So, what do you think of him?" he asked.

"He's a duck," she murmured, smiling wistfully as she hugged him close and rocked him. "A sweet little baby duck. I don't ever want to put him down."

He nodded. "He looks pretty good to me, too. As long as he's not crying."

She flashed a startled look at the tall man beside her. She'd had dealings with a man who was irrationally bothered by a baby crying. It wasn't a good thing. But she calmed down immediately. After all, what he'd said was probably a common complaint.

"Who is he?" she asked, stroking the hair on his little head. "What's the connection?"

He hesitated, then decided he might as well tell the truth. "He's my brother's child," he said. "At least, that's the assumption. We'll find out after DNA testing is done."

She drew back. Something didn't sit well with her. All the sense of well-being brought on by holding this baby seemed to melt away quickly.

"He's your brother's baby and you've never seen him before?" She frowned, searching his face for clues.

He shrugged. "I've been in Italy," he said, as though that explained everything.

She made a face. "Where's your brother? Or the baby's mother, for that matter?"

"Good question." He decided to ignore the part about his brother. "We don't know. She seems to have disappeared. The babysitter said she should have been back days ago."

She nodded, taking that in. "So I guess you're going to call the police?"

Without missing a beat, he said firmly, "No. Not yet."

"But…"

He moved impatiently. "Listen C.J., this is really none of your affair. I've been involved in the search for this baby for weeks now. We've finally found him and we'll do what we think necessary."

She shook her head, exasperated. "Why do you keep calling me that?" she asked. "My name is Cari. It's a fine name and it doesn't need shortening to C.J."

He raised a dark eyebrow. "A little formal, isn't it? You actually want me to call you Miss Kerry all the time?"

"No." He was such an annoying man. "Drop the 'miss'. I'm not a Southern belle."

He looked puzzled. "Let me get this straight. You want to be called by your last name?"

"Cari isn't my last name," she interjected quickly. "I don't know where you got that idea. It's my given name. Just plain Cari. And there's no *J* involved at all."

He shook his head, bewildered by that. "Your name is Celinia Jade Kerry, right?"

"No." She wrinkled her nose in distaste at the silly name he was trying to pin on her. "My name is Cari Christensen. That's been my name for quite some time now. In fact, it's official, and I've got proof. Want to see my driver's license?"

He stared into her clear blue eyes for a long moment. She certainly looked like a woman telling the absolute truth. The light began to dawn. Something had been a little off about this entire operation from the start. She hadn't fit the profile he was expecting. He should have trusted his instincts. And now—what the hell had he done? This was the wrong woman.

"Uh-oh," he said at last.

CHAPTER THREE

CARI sighed, impatience building ever higher as she hugged the baby to her chest. This date had been strange from the start, but it was getting stranger.

First this man had turned out to be so incredibly different from what she'd expected. Then there was the Italian element—not to mention the accent. The mother on the phone. Abandoned babies in dirty apartments. An assistant named Tito. If she hadn't known better, she might think she'd landed in the middle of a scene from a bad B movie and was caught up in some really crazy dialogue. Mara had not forewarned her of all of this.

"Listen, Randy," she began, eyes flashing as she prepared to read him the riot act.

His own eyes widened and his head went back. "Who the hell is Randy?" he demanded.

Shock jolted through her. This man wasn't Randy? This man wasn't the one she'd been waiting for, the one her friend had set her up with? This wasn't her blind date?

But of course he wasn't. Hadn't she suspected that

all along? The scales fell from her eyes—so to speak. This wasn't Mara's husband's cousin after all. And that just about explained everything.

"Aren't you Randy Jeffington?" she asked, though by now she knew darn well he wasn't.

He shook his head, looking like a man who expected all things in his path to snap into place and had been sorely disappointed once again—a man who was planning to make sure someone paid for this.

"Never heard of him," he growled at her.

"Uh-oh," she echoed softly, swaying and feeling just a bit unsteady on her feet.

Suddenly she had a clear and shining picture of a tall, sandy-haired man in glasses carrying a red rose. She'd seen him just as they were leaving the club and she now had an epiphany. That, no doubt, was Randy. Poor guy.

But something in the back of her mind had known all along, hadn't it? This handsome figure standing before her was just too good to be true. Or too bad, as the case might be.

And poor Randy Jeffington. Was he still wandering around the Longhorn Lounge looking for her? Her hand went to her mouth, her eyes huge.

"Omigosh. We've got to go back."

He nodded grimly. "You've got that right. We've got the wrong dates."

"There must be a woman named…whatever that weird name you said was…waiting for you back there."

"Holding a red rose."

"Oh, no." She grimaced tragically. "Too bad we all picked the same color, isn't it?"

He was still glowering at her. "Too bad we didn't get identities straight from the beginning," he said curtly.

She frowned, shifting the baby from one hip to the other and trying to remember how it had happened. "You called me Miss Cari. My name is Cari, with a *C*. I thought—"

"I called you Miss Kerry with a *K*."

"Oh. Well, it was hard to know that at the time."

"It was perfectly straightforward. You should have guessed."

"*I* should have guessed? What about *you?* You acted like you were sure I was the one. I sort of just… followed along—like a dummy." She frowned, remembering how she'd almost been in a trance. She could hardly believe that a man like this was the Randy she was waiting for. And it turned out she was right. She sighed plaintively.

"Oh, well. What's done is done. Now we have to do our best to undo it."

"Exactly." He glanced down at the sleeping baby in her arms, then around the simple room. "Let's get out of here."

She looked down at the baby. "Are we taking him with us?"

"Well, we're not going to leave him here."

"No, I suppose not." She bit her lip. This didn't seem right, but she didn't know what else they could do.

From the crib, she picked up a blanket and wrapped it around the baby while he picked up the diaper bag. Looking up, she sighed as her gaze traveled over the handsome man who'd brought her here. He was like a mythic figure, so tall and strong with matinee-idol looks. When something seemed too good to be true, you had to know it was likely to be so. Oh well, this had been interesting.

"So what is your name, anyway?" she asked as they looked around the apartment to make sure they weren't forgetting anything.

"Max," he said grimly. "Max Angeli."

"And I'm Cari Christensen."

He looked down at her and almost had to smile. She seemed to be able to maintain a sunny personality despite all odds against it. In contrast to what he was feeling himself, which was dour indeed. "You said that."

"I thought you might not have caught it in the heat of the moment."

He nodded, mouth twisting. "I wish you'd mentioned it while we were still at the club," he said. "There you were waving at me with that damn red rose."

"Oh!" She stopped and glared at him. "You're not going to blame this whole catastrophe on me."

He liked the fire in her eyes. She wasn't his type and he would never have picked her out of a crowd, but there was something appealing about her just the same. He liked the liveliness of her reactions and he couldn't resist teasing her a bit.

"Why not?" he said with a careless shrug. "If you'd been on your toes, this wouldn't have happened. You made me stand up the woman I was supposed to be with. You may have killed that relationship."

"And you messed up my date with Randy," she reminded him, though she was beginning to realize he wasn't really serious.

"Wasn't it a blind date?" he asked her as they headed out of the apartment. He turned back to make sure the door was locked. "And you know what they say about love."

"I know they say love is blind, but I think you have to give it a chance to grow before you can kill it."

"Murderess," he muttered, choking back a smile.

She sighed, glancing at him sideways. "You're not exactly the Lone Ranger, my friend," she chided, teasing him back now. "For all you know, you may have destroyed a great love affair."

He raised a skeptical eyebrow. "You and Randy?"

"Sure. Why not?" She made a face at him. "Romeo and Juliet. Anthony and Cleopatra. Debbie Reynolds and Eddie Fisher." She struck a pose. "The names Cari and Randy might have belonged right up there with them all."

"All doomed to tragedy," he noted helpfully. "If a great passion is meant to be it'll take more than a missed connection to destroy it."

"Perhaps." She flashed him a smile. "And yours, too."

His laugh was short and humorless. "C.J. and I aren't

meant for love," he said cynically. "But we are destined to make beautiful music together."

She looked at him with bewilderment. "How can you know that when you don't even know who she is?"

He knew enough about C.J. to know she was meant—unfortunately—to be very important in his life. He might not know what she looked like, but he had her number, just the same. His smile was bittersweet as he shrugged, pushing open the outer door to the building for her.

"Destiny is relentless."

"Destiny. Such a strong word."

But all that was forgotten as she looked at what they were heading into.

"It's starting to rain," she said with dismay, just as they stepped outside and the door clicked shut behind them.

"Yes," Max said, wondering what else could go wrong. Just another layer of bad luck he supposed. But this was getting monotonous.

"Where's the car?" she asked.

"The car?"

He looked where he'd parked it. The space was empty. His first thought was—did Tito take it? But no. He glanced at the driveway. Tito's rental car was gone. He looked back at the place where he'd left his newly minted beauty. Sure enough, it was gone, too. His heart sank. And now he knew what else could go wrong.

He swore coldly and obscenely, and she pulled the baby closer, frowning at him, even though the words were in Italian. Reaching into his pocket, he realized he'd left his mobile in the car, which had now been stolen. He swore again.

"Where's your phone?" he asked curtly.

She shook her head. "I forgot to bring it," she said.

He stared at her, unable to believe this string of bad luck wasn't over yet.

"My car's been stolen. You have no phone. I have no phone. We just locked ourselves out of the building and it's starting to rain."

She sighed, shoulders sagging. That was quite a litany of woes. "We're also stuck in the middle of a rather bad neighborhood," she reminded him, looking around at the menacing shadows.

"Not for long." He picked up the diaper bag and glanced down the street. The lights from downtown were visible in the sky. It was quite evident which way they needed to travel. "We're going to have to walk, at least until we can flag down a cab. Let's go. The sooner we start out, the sooner we'll get there."

Cari looked down at her three-inch heels. "Okay," she said sadly, trying to smile.

He looked down at them, too. "Those shoes aren't made for walking," he noted dryly.

That was certainly a fact, but her feet sure were cute in them, and what that angle did to her beautiful legs was beyond mentioning. He swallowed hard as the thought came and nestled into his senses. Raising his gaze to her clear blue eyes, he got another jolt of erotic sensation and he shook his head, trying to stave it off. This was no time to let his libido go wild.

"I could carry you," he said gruffly, still holding her gaze with his own. "But with the baby and all…"

"You will not!" she retorted, taking a step away from him. "I can walk. Believe me, I've done it for years." She started off down the street, just to prove it. "I'll carry the baby. You get the diaper bag. It's heavier."

They set off into the dark neighborhood, trying to ignore the drizzle. Most of the buildings seemed to be industrial and there was no sign of life coming from any that lined the street they were hurrying down. It was downright spooky.

Max pushed all thought about his beautiful Ferrari out of his mind. There was no point in mourning over a car when he had so many other things to worry about. An occasional driver went by, driving too fast to be flagged down, and there were no people out on the street—at least, none that made their presence known. But there was an eerie feeling, a sort of vague menace. This was not the sort of neighborhood either one of them would have wandered into voluntarily. Bad things tended to happen at night in areas like this.

Cari was feeling the creepiness as well, and instinctively she held the baby closer. Looking down, she felt a quick surge of tenderness for the child. Babies should be protected from harm and that was what adults where there for. But just as she had that thought, a flash of pain sliced through her. If only she'd been able to protect her own baby from harm. If only Brian had been more careful. If only…

No. She shook the regrets away. She'd been down that road so many times. Right after the accident that took her husband and her baby, she'd spent months almost drowning in recriminations, all the old "if only" cries of the heart. It had taken time and a bit of counseling to help her pull out of that downward spiral and she never wanted to take a plunge like that again. You could either immerse yourself in the past and die bit by bit, or reach out to the future and make a new life. Slowly, painfully, she was trying to do the latter.

But for now the past was useful in the training she'd had with her own baby. She seemed to bond naturally with this one, and that felt better than she had any right to expect.

So she looked over her shoulder, wishing they were in a better neighborhood.

"Do you have a weapon with you?" she asked Max, not really expecting him to answer in the affirmative, just expressing trepidation.

"Unfortunately, I forgot to bring my Glock," he quipped, but she noticed he took a quick look over his shoulder as well. "If only I'd known I'd need it."

"There you go," she said lightly. "I guess you were never a Boy Scout."

He gave her a long sideways look. "What would that have done for me?"

She shrugged her free shoulder and pulled the baby

more closely to the other one. "You'd have known about their motto. Be Prepared."

"Oh, I'm prepared."

"Still, you're not a real Texan, are you?" She sighed, pretending it was such a pity.

That was meant to get his goat and it did the job.

"I'm Italian," he said with quick native pride. "That's just as good, you know." He grunted. "On second thought, it's better."

"Is it?" She gave him a mockingly taunting look. "From what I hear, Italians are pretty emotional, compared to Texans. They talk real fast, yell a lot, say outlandish things."

"Sort of like Texans?" He got the joke, but he grinned and played along. "Why not? We enjoy life more than most people do. What's more, we're warm, loyal and generous to a fault." His voice dropped in a husky way that was meant to make her senses quiver. "And we're the most passionate lovers on earth."

She was glad the darkness hid how hot her cheeks suddenly became. The surge of warmth surprised her. She'd fallen for this guy's good looks and masculinity from the first, but in a reserved way, the way she dealt with most of life. She usually didn't let emotions— or even attractions—down into her inner core. Her heart was protected by a thick wall of experience, not much of it good. Had she actually allowed this handsome Italian to get to her? She couldn't let that happen.

"Well, good for you," she said as lightly as she could manage. "I guess Miss C. J. Kerry will be glad to hear it."

He frowned, not pleased to be reminded of the mess this evening had turned into. He wasn't happy that he'd done anything to put Celinia Jade Kerry in a hostile mood. He needed her happy and compliant. The woman might be short on cash, but to a female, a sense of having been overlooked and ignored for another could blot all that out. He was going to have to be very tactful with the lady—tactful and apologetic.

Still, the night wasn't a total loss at all. They had found Gino's baby. Just an hour before, he hadn't been sure there really was a baby. And now Jamie was in Cari's arms and on his way to a complete medical checkup and a DNA test.

The fact that baby Jamie's mother was missing disturbed him, and yet it made things easier in the short run. Eventually, he had no doubt they would find her. For just a moment he imagined what it would be like for his mother when he returned to Venice with Gino's baby in tow—and hopefully, the deed to her family ranch in hand. Maybe that would erase some of the sadness from her eyes and bring back just a touch of joy to her life. That had been his goal from the start of this adventure. His mother's happiness meant a lot to him.

Lost in thought, he didn't notice the small group of nasty neighborhood thugs until they stepped out in front of them, blocking their way. The effect on his danger radar was immediate, though. He stopped Cari and the baby with an outstretched arm, putting his body between her and the three gang-bangers.

"What do you want?" he barked at them.

"I don't know, man," one of them sneered. Tall and thin, he wore a red bandanna tied tightly around his head. "What you got?"

"Nothing that will do you any good," he said. "Let us pass."

The one who had spoken before gave an ugly laugh. "No way," he said, and suddenly there was the flash of a knife in his hand.

Max stared at the knife, knowing this was not good. What a night. This, on top of all the rest, just about did it for him. How much bad luck could one night bring? Fed up, he let his inner Italian take over. Moving toward the men in an aggressive rather than a defensive manner, he began to curse loud and long, in Italian, shouting at the men, shaking his fist at them for good measure. Instead of allowing himself to be the victim, *he* was threatening *them*.

Cari watched, her heart in her throat, fear sizzling through her. From every advice column she'd ever read, this seemed to be exactly the wrong way to go about this and she knew it. This could end very badly. But in the meantime, what could she do? Should she run? Not in these shoes. There was no chance. Everything in her wanted to protect the baby. But the way Max was acting, she was very much afraid she was going to see the knife slashing into his chest any moment.

And then what?

Still, it didn't seem to be playing out quite the way she'd expected. To her surprise, the shortest of the men was pulling on the arm of the one with the knife.

"Hold on," he was saying. "Just hold up, dude. Look at the guy."

"Hey, get a load of that suit," the third was saying nervously. "And listen to the way he talks. I think he's Mafia, dude. You don't want to screw with those guys."

"Mafia?" The three of them stared hard at Max who was still cursing. "Hey, they can mess you up bad."

"It's not worth it, dude," the one with the knife said at last, backing away. "Let's get out of here."

And they vanished as suddenly as they had appeared.

Max and Cari both stood very still, letting the adrenaline slow down, getting their breathing back to normal.

"Is that it?" she said at last.

"It seems to be," he responded. He turned and came back quickly, taking her by the shoulders and staring down into her eyes. "Are you okay?" he asked intensely.

She nodded, still too shaken to say much. Being almost mugged by thugs was enough to ruin a perfectly good evening walk, but watching Max explode like a smoldering volcano had been almost as shocking. She'd never seen a man do that before.

"Good." He let out a long breath. "We're lucky they gave up so easily."

She nodded, finally finding her voice. "Wow, I guess you don't need a weapon after all," she said, looking at him with reluctant admiration.

He brushed it off. He knew how to handle himself and he'd been pretty confident, even with three men opposing him, until he'd seen the knife. That could change everything. Luckily, they had weighed the odds and decided not to risk annoying the mob.

Though that made him want to smile. Some people thought anyone Italian had ties to gangsters. That was an ignorant assumption, but it had come in handy this time.

"Okay, let's go. We've got to get out of this neighborhood. Places like this seem to breed thugs like rats thriving in the shadows. Let's head for streets that are better lit. That way I think." He pointed down another street and they headed in that direction, moving quickly.

Her feet were aching, but she ignored it. She'd go barefoot if she had to. Anything to get out of this part of town.

"Hold tight to the baby," Max ordered suddenly, slinging the diaper bag up over his shoulder.

She looked up, startled, and the next thing she knew, he'd bent to slide support under her legs and was swinging her up into his arms, baby and all. She squeaked in protest, but he ignored her.

"You're going to trip in those shoes," he told her. "I can handle it. Just hold on."

She held on and somehow, it worked. He cradled them both in a warm, muscular embrace and walked firmly along the wet sidewalk. She clung to the space just above his chest and beneath his chin and closed her eyes, reveling in the sense of his masculine strength. His heart was beating against her shoulder. She let herself fall into a sort of daze, listening to the rhythm and soaking up the whole of him.

He moved quickly, wondering how he'd let himself get into this insane situation. She was light as a feather, despite the added weight of the baby, and she smelled like a garden in sunshine. Strands of her blond hair flew up and tickled his nose, which he found tantalizing rather than annoying. All in all, she was warm and soft and round and he felt like a Neanderthal. He wanted to take her home and keep her—preferably in his bed.

This wasn't right. She wasn't meant for him. In fact, he had other fish to fry, and he was late for the barbecue. But she seemed so small and vulnerable in his arms and he couldn't resist filling his head with her fresh, intoxicating scent.

A few steps more and they were around the corner, and suddenly cars were whizzing past and the streetlights actually lit up the street instead of just muddying the atmosphere.

"Civilization," Max muttered, lowering Cari to the ground carefully and looking up and down the road. "But still no cabs."

And more rain. Thunder rolled and the heavens opened up.

"This way, quickly," he shouted, pulling her and the baby along until he got them under the limited protection of an empty bus stop shelter. They dashed inside and quickly clung together, trying to stay out of the spray, as water poured off the rounded roof of the tiny kiosk, shooting all around them. After the first moment or two, Cari looked up and realized just how close they were standing. Her nose almost touched his chin.

"Oh," she said, thinking she should pull back. Being this close when she was being carried was one thing, but this was ridiculous.

"No." Reaching out, he held the two of them against his chest. "You'll just get wet."

"But…" She bit her lip, not sure what to say or where to look.

"Don't worry," he said, his voice so low she could hardly hear it over the rain. "I don't bite."

"Don't you?" She heard herself say the words and winced, knowing they sounded almost as though she were flirting. She hadn't meant to do that.

The way his mouth twisted in a half grin let her know he'd heard it that way, too. "I suppose I could be convinced," he said softly.

She gazed into his dark eyes and somehow couldn't look anywhere else. The sound of the rain, the momentary isolation, the way they were pressed so closely, all blended together to weave an enchantment around them. He was going to kiss her. She could see it in his eyes. And if she didn't watch out, she was going to end up kissing him back.

"No," she murmured, trying to dredge up the strength to resist.

"Yes," he countered, lowering his lips to hers.

"No," she said again, shaking her head.

"Why not?" he asked, so close to her.

"The baby…"

"The baby's asleep. He can't see a thing."

"This is all wrong." Looking up, she searched his eyes. "We're not even supposed to be on this date."

"This isn't a date," he said, his own eyes deep and smoky with something nameless that set her pulse pounding. "It's an encounter. A moment in time." He dropped a quick kiss on her lips. "A bit of magic. You'll forget all about it by morning."

"I don't think so," she said with a sigh. "You really shouldn't…"

"But I want to," he said huskily. "And you taste so good."

And then he took her mouth with his and kissed her like she'd never been kissed before.

CHAPTER FOUR

IN THE harsh and revealing sunlight of morning, it all looked a bit fantastical. Cari buried her face in her pillow and wished she'd done a better job pulling together the drapes on her tall windows before she'd gone to sleep. She wasn't ready to face reality yet. Did last night really happen? Impossible.

The phone rang, but she let the answering machine take it. Her heart thumped as she waited for the voice she knew was coming.

"Cari?"

Yes. It was Max. His deep baritone sent chills all through her system. She drew in a shuddering breath.

"Go away," she whispered into the empty air.

"Cari? Surely you are there. I wouldn't bother you so early, but I need a bit of advice. If you could pick up…"

She knew she shouldn't pick up. In her sleepy, morning state, she imagined herself standing at a fork in the road. Her life could go one way or the other, depending on what she did in the next few moments.

She knew what she should do. She should mark the whole experience from the night before as lessons learned and move on. She had to ignore him. Go back to real life and not fool around with fairy-tale princes who came breezing in from Italy with a knowing smile and a boatload of hunkiness. She shouldn't pick up. She knew better. She wasn't going to do it.

"Cari? Please?"

She writhed beneath her covers. Don't do it, Cari!

"Cari, it's about the baby."

The baby? Well, if it was about the baby…

"Cari?"

With a sigh she reached out and picked up.

"Hello," she said somewhat mournfully.

"Buongiorno," he responded.

There was a long pause while neither of them said anything. Cari wondered if he was as hesitant about this as she was. After all, last night it had been assumed they would probably never see each other again. Hadn't it?

He'd kissed her and she'd swooned. Yes, there was no way to deny it. She'd gone all gaga on him. Luckily a cab had come cruising up before she'd made a complete fool out of herself, and they'd piled in and raced back to the Longhorn Lounge where they'd found Tito waiting anxiously. The two dates they should have been with were long gone, of course. That was only natural. Tito then left for the hotel with the baby while Max headed for the police station to make a stolen car report. And

Cari had slipped into her own car and turned toward home, still tingling. Still swooning. Still out of her mind!

But pretty darn sure she would never see or hear from him again. After all, their little—what had he called it? Their encounter? Whatever it was, it had been illegitimate in the first place. Time to wipe it out of her life and her mind.

Only, here he was on the telephone.

"How did you find my number?" she asked at last.

"I have people on my staff who can find these things for me."

"Oh."

She supposed he meant Tito. Or were there others? Hmm. She wasn't sure she liked that.

"How is he?" she asked.

"Who? The baby?"

"Yes."

"Okay."

"Has his mother shown up?"

"No. I've got someone monitoring the apartment periodically, just in case."

"Good." She couldn't imagine what could have kept a mother away from that beautiful baby. "But you said there was some sort of problem?" she asked quickly. That was what she'd picked up for, after all.

"Not exactly a real problem," he said. "But…I've hired a live-in nanny."

"Oh. Well, good. You checked her references?"

"Of course."

She let out a long breath. She didn't let herself think a lot about the baby she'd held so closely the night before. That was all a part of that other fork in the road she wasn't going to take—even if she had picked up the phone.

"Okay, then."

She waited. He had something else to say, but he was having trouble getting it out. She could picture him looking thoughtful, brow furrowed, then she blinked that image away. If she kept doing that sort of thing, she would be swooning again.

"Max, what is it?"

"Nothing, really, it's just that…" He sighed. "Listen, I'm just not sure about this nanny thing. I did the regular vetting, but what the hell do I know about nannies? Or babies, for that matter. And you seem to know a lot. So I thought maybe you could come over and see if you think she knows what she's doing."

Wow. He needed her. That was almost enough to get those tingles started again. Everything in her wanted to say yes. She cared about the baby, but there was more. To see him again, be with him doing something important, wouldn't that be ideal? But no, that would be wrong—on so many levels. So she didn't say yes.

"No," she said instead. Then she waited for the rush of self-congratulations that would surely follow. Funny, but that didn't happen. "I'm sorry, Max," she went on, falling back on the honest truth. "I've got to go to work."

"Work? You work?"

It almost made her smile to realize how little they knew about each other. They'd shared a night of intense emotions and setbacks, more in one night than she'd had in months. She felt as if she'd glimpsed a clear picture of his character, his personality. And yet she didn't know much about him, what he'd done with his life, what he cared about, and he didn't know those things about her, either. But they were going to leave it that way for the most part. At least, she knew they should.

"Of course I work. What do you think I live on? Air?"

"What do you do?"

He sounded candidly surprised and interested. What the heck? Didn't he know any women who actually had real jobs? She licked her lips and stuck to the facts.

"I'm a waitress."

"At a supper club?"

"No. In a local coffee shop."

There. That ought to be guaranteed to turn him off. She was just a waitress. Not one of those high-falutin', jet-settin' fashion models he was surely used to.

She was also the assistant manager and studying for her real estate license, but he didn't need to know all that. After all, she wasn't trying to impress him. She was trying to get rid of him.

"Take a day off," he said bluntly.

"I can't do that. People are counting on me."

"And I'm counting on you, too."

"Yes, but you don't pay the bills."

"I could do that," he said, as though it was a new idea and he rather liked it. "That's it. I'll pay you a salary. I'll hire you."

"Nonsense." Her voice was quivering a bit and she bit down on her lip. No! She was not going to give in to that sort of crazy temptation.

"But it would be perfect."

"For you, not for me."

"No?"

"No."

"Consider it, at least."

"No." She was firm. And darn proud of herself, too. "You'll be fine with this nanny person."

He hesitated, then said skeptically, "I hope you're right."

There was another long pause.

"Everything is all right, then?" she prodded. "I mean, everything else?"

"Oh, yes. Going great. I had the baby checked out by a pediatrician first thing, and we've put in a request for a DNA test. I've arranged for the delivery of the relevant charts from Italy. It will all take time, but everything is moving along."

"Good."

Why was he still hanging on? She was torn, wanting him gone, yet enjoying this more than she ought to. "Well, have you gotten in touch with your date from last night yet?" she asked, suddenly remembering there was still that issue to be dealt with.

There was yet another hesitation, then he answered, "Not yet. How about you?"

She sighed. Apologizing to Randy wasn't something she was looking forward to. "No, not yet. But it's early. I wouldn't want to wake him up."

Something in the pause this time was electric, and finally he said softly, "Did I wake you?"

Warmth flooded her body. How did he manage to make one simple question imply a wealth of intimate contact? Something in his tone, the low, husky quality of his voice, conjured up a picture of the way he might awaken her, his hand sliding down beneath the sheets, his lips leaving a trail of hot kisses. She suppressed a gasp.

This was ridiculous. She wasn't a schoolgirl. She was a grown woman. She'd been married, for heaven's sake! She knew what it was like to have a man in her bed.

But not this man. Oh, my!

She wasn't going to answer his provocative question. She had to think of something else, quick. Something to break the mood and put an end to this.

"I've been up for hours," she lied shamelessly. "I've got a life, you know. Things to do. Places to go."

"And you'd like to get back to it," he said softly, taking the hint. He sighed. "All right, Cari. I'll let you go."

Her fingers were so tight on the receiver, they were beginning to ache. "Thanks."

"So that's it, then."

She blinked, suddenly feeling almost weepy. "It seems to be."

"It was nice knowing you, Cari."

"Yes. Same here." Now her eyes were definitely stinging. Ridiculous! "Goodbye."

"*Ciao.*"

She hung up, said a word she hardly ever said, and threw a stuffed animal against the wall.

Cari was just finishing up a bowl of morning cereal when Mara called.

"So," said Mara brightly. "How was it?"

"How was what?" Cari answered, her mind still stuck on mulling over her conversation with Max.

"The date with Randy."

"Oh. Uh…" She grimaced, putting her spoon into the bowl and pushing it away across the counter. "Well, actually, we didn't have it."

"What do you mean you didn't have it? Don't tell me you chickened out?"

Mara's voice was sharp with what was fast working into a sense of outrage. Cari tried to nip that in the bud.

"No, Mara, I did not chicken out. I was there with bells on. And I waited for quite some time. But then…" She sighed. This really wasn't all that easy to explain. "Well, I kind of went off with the wrong man."

"What?" There was still an edge to Mara's voice. "How did you do that, exactly?"

"Believe me, it was not that hard. Not when he came up carrying a red rose, just like you told *me* to do for Randy, and he seemed to call me by my name and…

and…" She sighed. "It's kind of hard to explain. Listen, I've got the lunch shift. I'll swing by on my way to work. We'll talk."

"I guess. Okay."

Mara sounded grumpy. Cari knew she was disappointed. She thought she'd planned the perfect date for a good friend and it had all gone wrong. Who wouldn't be disappointed? And Mara had been so excited. She groaned internally. But she would take care of things when she stopped by her friend's house. Face-to-face it might actually be possible to give her a better picture of exactly what had happened.

"In the meantime, uh, do you have Randy's number?"

She was tempted to put it off for a while, but she steeled herself and called the man. Once she had him on the phone and explained who she was, he reacted well. Instead of demanding an explanation, he was apologetic that he'd been a little late.

Which only made her feel more guilty. It was hard to explain why she'd dumped him for some suave Italian guy. There was no good excuse for it, actually. One look into Max's deep dark eyes had mesmerized her and she'd been ready to follow him anywhere. But how could she tell Randy that?

"Well, it was certainly an interesting evening," he said. "I haven't had many like that."

He sounded just as likable as Mara had said. She was impressed that he didn't seem at all disgruntled. She had a quick flashback to how her husband, Brian, would have reacted to what had happened, and the memory of his volatile temper made her cringe.

"Did you wait for long?"

"Only for an hour or so." He chuckled. "Actually, I met the woman who was supposed to be dating the man you ran off with."

"Ran off with" seemed a bit harsh, but she let it go. After all, the man deserved a little dig here and there, didn't he? He'd paid his dues.

"Oh. C.J.?"

"Celinia Jade. Do you know her?"

"No, I don't, but Max told me something about her."

"Well, she's somethin' else."

His voice conveyed a sense of awe. Cari tensed a bit.

"Is she?"

"Oh, yeah. She's dynamite."

For some reason, that didn't make her smile. She chewed on her lip and wondered if Max was going to be as impressed with the woman once they got together. But what did that matter, anyway? Grimacing, she avoided the impulse to slap herself.

"We were both wandering around with red roses," Randy went on. "So we started talking. It didn't take us long to figure out what must have happened. So we hung out for a while, sort of commiserated, so to speak." He chuckled again. "She had some funny stories to tell. That passed the time for a while. But when y'all didn't come back, we called it a night and headed home."

She nodded. It sounded like he'd enjoyed the evening

with C.J. as much as he might have with her. Maybe more. She frowned at the trend in her own thoughts.

"So it wasn't a total waste," she said quickly.

"Oh, no, not at all."

"Well, would you like to try it again tonight?" she said, knowing she pretty much had to suggest it. "I sort of promised Mara I would."

"I guess we both promised Mara, didn't we?"

"She can be persuasive."

"Oh, yes." He chuckled again. He seemed a happy sort. "Let's do it," he agreed. "Only this time, why don't I pick you up at your place? I'm not sure that red rose thing works very well."

She hesitated. The rationale for meeting at the club had been to avoid letting a strange man know where she lived. She was wary these days. She didn't want to risk any man getting the upper hand in a relationship. But he seemed so genuinely nice, she decided it wouldn't hurt to give him her address.

Maybe all would go great. Maybe she and Randy would get along so well, the crazy night with Max would be forgotten, a relic of history, a strange interlude in what she was hoping to turn into a sensible, placid life. Maybe.

Max was restless. He'd spent the afternoon hovering over the nanny, second-guessing everything she did. She'd snapped at him once, and he'd almost fired her. But he'd quickly realized that he had no replacement lined up. If she left, he would be on his own. And what he knew about taking care of babies could be blurted out in one quick epithet.

Tito was no help. Every time the baby cried, he stuffed cotton in his ears and went out on the hotel room balcony, plunked himself down into a plastic chair and tried to sleep. But Max couldn't sleep. His existence was caught up in this baby for now, and that was all he could think about.

That, and Cari Christensen. She was the one person he knew who could help solve a lot of his problems. But he had to forget about her.

He'd come to Dallas with two clear goals in mind. First, he'd wanted to find Sheila and discover if the baby she claimed she had was really Gino's. That was pretty much in the works. He had no idea where Sheila was, but when you came right down to it, that didn't matter. He had the baby. And he would soon know the truth about the baby's parentage.

He'd never been a baby person, never been around the little things. And he hadn't expected to feel much of anything for this one. Babies were nothing but potential people—little blobs of flesh and noise. Puppies had more personality.

But the funny thing was, he'd felt something of an instant connection when he'd seen baby Jamie. One look at that little face had torn a hole in his heart. He was as sure of this as anything—this baby was his brother's.

When word had come that Gino had died in the crash

of the plane he was testing out, Max had felt his world tilt on its axis. His big brother had been his guiding star all his life. For a long time, he'd thought he might never feel joy again.

But he'd had to suppress any overt mourning, because his mother's despair had been so deep and so complete it had taken all his effort to pull her out of what he was afraid could have developed into a suicidal impulse at any moment. And now, to think he might be able to bring her Gino's baby—the thought took his breath away. He couldn't allow himself to get too invested in this until the tests proved the connection. But he was pretty sure what the results would be.

His other goal had been to find a way to wrest the Triple M Ranch from the daughter of his mother's old rival. That wasn't going so well. But he hadn't really concentrated on it as yet, so there was plenty of time to figure out ways to succeed there, too. He'd contacted Celinia Jade, or C.J. as he preferred to call her—and she didn't seem to mind—who came across as something of an airhead at first. But in no time at all, he'd noticed a sharp turn of mind that sent up warning flags. The woman might talk like she had nothing in her mind but fluff, but underneath there was a steely sense of purpose. She knew what she wanted, and she wasn't going to be easy to snow. He might have more trouble there than he'd anticipated.

They had made plans to try to meet again tonight, same time, same place. This time he was going to make damn sure he had the right woman. No more screwups.

He was going to be pure Mediterranean charm and so-licitude. The woman wouldn't know what hit her.

He knew what he was doing. His life for the past ten years had been immersed in real estate—big real estate, big deals. This was nothing. It should be a piece of cake. C.J. was in financial trouble and he planned to make a very nice offer for the ranch. He was prepared to be fair, generous, even. He wasn't out to cheat any-one. His mother seemed to think emotional ties would make it hard for her to sell, but he had his doubts. When faced with the facts, he was pretty sure he would be able to make her see the light.

If he could return to Italy with the deed to the ranch in one hand and Gino's baby in the other, some of the heartbreak that shadowed his mother's eyes might fade a bit. That was his hope.

The baby was crying again. He paced the floor for a few minutes, then gave in to the urge to go into the nursery they had rigged up in the smallest bedroom of this lavish hotel suite and see what was going on. Mrs. Turner, the nanny, was sitting in the rocking chair, reading a mystery novel. Meanwhile, Jamie was turning bright red as he cried his little heart out.

"The baby's crying," he pointed out sharply.

Mrs. Turner looked up and nodded, glaring at him. "It's good for him to cry. It develops his lungs."

He was nothing if not skeptical, but he hesitated. "Really?"

"Absolutely." She gave him the supercilious smirk he

was growing to hate. "Why else would they have that ability?"

He gritted his teeth. "I thought it was so they could let people know they needed help."

She smiled as though he were a poor fool who knew nothing about children. "That's only part of it. You can't baby them, you know. You mustn't spoil them, even at the infant stage. It's best to encourage them to grow and stretch themselves. You wouldn't want the poor dear to fall behind in development, now would you?"

He wanted to argue, but he had no ammunition. What did he know about this, anyway?

"I suppose you know best," he grumbled, turning away. But the picture of Jamie's little tragic face, all twisted with grief, staying in his mind.

Back out in the living room, he went to the folder where he was keeping his papers and pulled out the certificate that was meant to guarantee the expertise of the nanny. Maybe he should give the school that issued it a call. He frowned. Or maybe he should just call Cari and see what she thought.

His hand was already on the telephone receiver when he stopped himself. No, he couldn't do that. He had to break all ties with the woman. That was the only way he would ever get her out of his head. He couldn't let himself think about Cari and her sweet, pretty face. He'd set his sights on charming C.J. and that was where they had to stay. Swearing, he reached for the cotton to put in his ear and started out to join Tito on the balcony.

* * *

The Copper Penny where Cari worked was just off the interstate. A mix of locals and tourists patronized the trim little café. She liked the early afternoon when the hectic lunch crowd had dwindled down to a few house-wives lingering over coffee and the assorted cowboys who came in from riding fences at some of the nearby ranches. The easy camaraderie was what she liked best about her job. It was pretty much the same group of cowhands that came in every day. One by one, most had tried to hit on her, but in a relaxed, friendly way that never got serious. She could swat their propositions aside like a mama dog controlling her puppies. Few took offense, and those that did were easily joked out of it.

Today Cari wasn't doing any joking. Her mind was on other things and she poured coffee and took orders with a distracted air. The men she served were a blur to her. Her thoughts were full of Max.

"I've just got to think about him as much as I can now, so I can be done with him and get him out of my head," she told herself impatiently. It was a plan, but she wasn't at all sure it was a plan that was going to work.

She'd known from the moment he'd walked into the club that he was absolutely the wrong man for her. Too tall, too handsome, too arrogant, too sure of his right to command the attention of everyone there.

Her husband had been like that in a way. Well, not so tall, not so handsome, and not so full of self-confidence. But he'd had the arrogance down pat. Brian had mostly been frustrated in his attempts to take charge of the rest of the world. He'd had a bit more success in boxing her in with his small life and visions. And he'd managed to make her life miserable because of it.

The autocratic husband was the worst kind, as far as she was concerned. She wasn't sure she ever wanted another man in her life at all, but if she did decide to try another relationship, it sure wouldn't be with a man like Brian. Or Max, for that matter.

"That's why Randy is so perfect for you," Mara had pointed out when she'd stopped by to see her and try to explain how she'd ended up on a date with the wrong man. "You've really got to get to know him. You'll have to date him more than once to really give him a chance."

"Oh, Mara, I don't know. After what happened last night…"

"Listen, you owe it to him. The poor guy spent hours waiting for you at the club."

"No he didn't. Not from what he told me. And anyway, he should have left after half an hour or so. I would have."

"In fact, you did." Mara gave her an exasperated sigh. "He was so excited about meeting you, of course. And now he's got to be wondering what all that meant. You've got to be nice to him and really give him a chance."

Cari had to hold back a smile. Mara was pushing a little too hard for this. That meant she'd begun to doubt it was going to work out. Oh, well. Cari would give it a shot. That was all she could do.

A new customer had come in and was about to seat himself at the counter. When she turned and saw it was Max, she gasped and almost dropped the coffee urn she was carrying. He gave her a halfhearted grin and shrugged. She put down the coffee and caught her breath. She'd never imagined he might show up here.

He was wearing slacks that fit his muscular body like a glove, bulging in all the right places, and a silky white shirt open low at the neck. He hadn't shaved and his face looked stunningly sexy with a day's worth of dark beard.

"What are you doing here?" she demanded in a voice just above a whisper. She didn't bother to ask how he'd found out which of the city's hundreds of coffee shops she worked in. She knew his answer to that one. His people knew how to find these things out. Something told her he would always find her if he wanted to, and she wasn't sure if that was a promise or a threat.

Max looked at her in wonder. She had her thick blond hair tied back, but little curls were breaking free all around her face. She wore a stiff, starched uniform, baby-blue with white lacy trim and a white lacy apron, sensible white shoes and a perky little hat. She looked for all the world like an exceptionally adorable matron in a fantasy children's ward. He half expected to see friendly cartoon characters bouncing along behind her.

"I came because I need to talk to you," he said. "You're the only person I know who knows anything about babies."

"What's wrong?" she asked quickly, a tiny flare of alarm shivering through her. "Has something happened?"

"No, nothing. Jamie's fine. Just fine." Max hesitated. He knew he sounded defensive and that made him frown more fiercely.

"Then what's wrong?" She shook her head in bewilderment.

"Nothing. Well, something."

He shook his own head, trying to figure out how to express the discomfort he felt with the childcare he'd arranged without sounding like a candidate for a mental clinic. Maybe what he'd seen was normal. Maybe he was being a crank. But maybe, just maybe, Mrs. Turner was a lousy nanny. He just didn't know the answer.

He sank down into the stool at the counter and turned up the cup. She moved automatically, filling it with coffee.

"Explain," she demanded impatiently. "What are the symptoms?"

His beautiful hands with their long, tapered fingers curled around the cup. She watched him do it, fascinated. Everything about him seemed better, even the way he held a cup. But she didn't have time for any swooning this afternoon. This was all about the baby.

"Well?" she said.

"It's just…oh, hell." He looked up, appealing to her supposed expertise. "He's crying a lot."

Cari froze and looked at him quickly. Brian had hated it when their baby had cried. In fact, it seemed to drive him a bit crazy when it happened. Her heart beat a little faster, but she took a deep breath and forced herself to calm down. Max wasn't Brian. He hadn't said he couldn't stand it, just that it worried him.

Okay, start over again.

She nodded a little stiffly. A baby crying wasn't really unusual. But if it was happening to the point where Max was worried, she was going to delve into it a bit.

"No fever?"

"No, I don't think so."

"Gas?"

He made a face. "I don't know."

"Does the nanny hold him against her shoulder and pat or rub his back?"

He thought for a minute, then nodded. "I've seen her do that a time or two. But not for long." He frowned. "I don't trust the nanny. She's obsessed with making sure she doesn't spoil him. It's like she thinks we're raising a Spartan kid or something. She doesn't want to make him too comfortable, as if he'll get too soft if he's happy." He grimaced. "So she lets him cry."

Cari was sure he was exaggerating, so she didn't take him too seriously. She closed her eyes, thinking, then opened them again and shook her head.

"You know what it probably is? He misses his mom."

Max searched her eyes. To his relief, Cari was taking his worries seriously. She was frowning, thinking over her instant diagnosis. She looked down at him.

"Did you get in a good supply of formula?"

"Of course."

She nodded again, then her eyes widened. "Oh, maybe he was being breast fed. The formula might not agree with him. Maybe that's why he's crying."

He groaned, looking miserable. "But Cari, there's nothing I can do about that."

"Of course not. He'll just have to get used to the formula."

"How long will that take?"

She had a hard time holding back a smile. His face was a picture of tragic helplessness. He was a man of action. He wanted to do something to make everything better. But he was being told there was nothing he could do, and that was maddening to him.

"Of course, the best thing would be if the baby's mother came back. You haven't found her yet?" she asked, knowing it wouldn't be a welcome question at all.

He gave her a baleful look. "Why would I want to do that?"

She stared at him, hoping he was just being flip. "You know darn well you *have* to do that."

His sigh was impatient. "Yes, I know. I've got people looking into it. We'll find her."

She frowned. His "people" had been pretty good at finding out where she lived and worked, but she was pretty easy. A woman who went off without telling anyone where she was going was probably going to be a tougher case.

"I hope you really mean that. It's important. What if

she comes back and her baby's not in the apartment? Can you imagine how frightened she'll be?"

He looked at her as though she'd lost her bearings. "Cari, this is a mother who walked out and never looked back. What makes you think she'll care that much?"

"She's a mother. I know what that's like."

To think a woman could walk out on her baby was incomprehensible to her. She'd lost a baby once herself. It had almost destroyed her life. "You don't know why she disappeared. Maybe something happened." She shrugged, getting into her speculative mode.

"Maybe she was kidnapped. Maybe she's unconscious in some hospital somewhere. Maybe she bumped her head and has amnesia."

He grimaced, not buying a bit of it. "Or maybe she went on a hot date and forgot she had a baby waiting at home."

She swallowed hard, shocked he would say such a thing. The cynicism reminded her of some of the terrible things Brian would say, and she didn't want to think he might be anything like her husband.

"You don't have a very high opinion of women, do you?" she challenged.

He looked up as though surprised she was taking his offhanded remark seriously. "That's not the point. And yes, I have a very high opinion of women. Some women."

His mother. Whoopee. She was appalled.

"No matter what kept her away, when she comes back to her senses, she'll want to know where her baby is."

"That's probably true. For what it's worth." His wide

mouth tilted at the corners, but there was no humor in his dark eyes as he looked up at her. "You forget. I know Sheila. I never understood what Gino saw in her, and I was glad when they broke up. And I was the one who took her phone call when she tried to shake us down for money. I'm afraid that experience has made me a little cynical where Sheila is concerned."

There was certainly no point in arguing about this. He knew the woman. She didn't. But the baby needed to be protected. At the same moment she had that thought, so did he.

"Listen," he said, rising from the stool and moving toward her. "I can pay you double whatever you're making here. I could really use the help."

She shook her head with vigor. She couldn't even allow herself to imagine such a thing.

"No," she said firmly. "Never."

"Cari…" He took her hand in his and she stared down at those wonderful fingers. The nails were so even, so beautiful. He had hands like an artist. She could hardly breathe.

"Cari, listen. It wouldn't be for long. Just until the DNA testing is completed. Then I'll be taking him to Venice with me and I won't need you anymore."

Her gaze jerked up and met his. Did he have any idea what he'd just said? But she supposed he didn't look at it quite the way she did. She yanked her hand out of his and turned away.

I won't need you anymore.

Wasn't that just like a man? Oh!

"Max, you'd better leave. I've got work to do."

"Cari…"

"I'm serious. Go. I'm not going to work for you. Not ever."

"Not ever." He repeated it as though he couldn't believe she'd said that and turned to go, then looked back. "By the way, the police found my car. It was only a few blocks from where it was stolen and they didn't damage anything. So that's okay."

"I'm glad."

He nodded, then shrugged and turned to leave again.

"But Max."

He turned back, one eyebrow raised.

"Max, please take care of the baby. And find his mother. It's really important."

He was on the verge of pointing out that she could help make all that happen, but he bit his tongue, knowing it would be too much like begging.

"Okay, I'll take that under advisement."

"Good."

Their gazes caught and held. For a moment she was afraid he was going to come back and grab her and carry her out, just like he'd carried her the night before. But the moment passed and he gave a half shrug.

"I'd better go back and see what the nanny's up to," he said at last. "If she's trying to get Jamie to make his own bed, I'm throwing her out on her ear."

And then he turned and was gone.

CHAPTER FIVE

RANDY was the perfect match for Cari, just as Mara had insisted all along. He was good-looking in a salt-of-the-earth kind of way, tall with a slender build, friendly, with sandy hair neatly cut and combed, steady gray eyes, a nice smile and a warm attitude. Cari liked him and immediately found herself thinking of women she knew she could set him up with. Seemingly, he was perfect for a lot of people.

"Why didn't you say something when Max called you C.J.?" he asked, after she'd gone over exactly what had happened the night before.

"I had no idea what he was talking about. For all I knew, he was calling me Calamity Jane. That's pretty much what I felt like once I realized what we'd done."

He laughed. They had just been seated at a comfortable booth in the main dining room at the Longhorn Lounge. The atmosphere was pleasant, the servers attentive, and drinks were on the way. The scene was set for a lovely evening, and a lovely evening they would have. But that was all.

She'd gone on this date to make a friend happy, and that was as far as her commitment went. Shortly after the dinner was consumed, she would thank the man, shake his hand and go off into the sunset—alone. In the meantime, she was determined to be nice to Randy, if only to make up for the night before.

But she had to mentally kick herself to stop looking toward the door, hoping Max would make a sudden appearance. She'd already seen him once today, and that was one time too many.

"Well, it was all my fault," Randy was saying graciously. "When I got there I knew I was half an hour late. I was afraid you'd have gotten disgusted and left me flat. So when I saw a gal coming in with a red rose, I was thrilled. Only, I took one look and I just really couldn't believe it could be you."

Déjà vu all over again.

"Really? What was she like?"

"Gorgeous."

He said it like a man smitten, and she had to recoil, just a little. So he'd thought the woman he saw was too good to be true, had he? Funny. That was exactly what she'd thought when she saw Max for the first time. What a coincidence.

"Well, thank you very much," she said a bit tartly, pretending to take offense. He hurried, a bit clumsily, to reassure her.

"No, I mean, you're beautiful. Of course you're beautiful."

She knew she was actually looking pretty good tonight. She'd worn an electric-blue number with spaghetti straps and more cleavage showing than usual, and she'd topped it off with a cute little fake fur shrug that didn't cover much of anything. Then she'd let her hair tumble free around her shoulders. But from the look shining in Randy's eyes, she had a feeling her "pretty good" was nothing compared to C.J.'s "gorgeous."

"You're a lovely woman," he was saying. "But in a totally different way. This gal looked like one of those heiresses with the big hair and the fancy clothes and diamonds and all that. Like the Dallas of the old TV show rather than the Dallas I usually live in."

His gaze grew dreamy as he thought of her. Cari had to laugh, shaking her head.

"I must be quite a disappointment after all that," she noted dryly.

Randy was surely planning on coming back with more reassurances, but he didn't get the chance, as visitors were stopping by their table. Cari looked up right into Max's intense gaze. Her heart leaped and the room seemed to tilt, and for just a moment she wondered if she was imagining things.

I could get lost in those eyes, was the thought running through her mind. Lost and bewitched. Again.

At the same time, his gaze made a quick trip along the line of her low-cut dress, and he gave every indication of liking what he saw there. Suddenly she realized she'd worn it for just such a reaction from him. And only him. And that only made her more light-headed.

It took her a beat too long to realize there was someone with him. Someone with a head of sumptuous red hair and a rather annoyed look on her beautiful face.

"So I guess we got it right this time," Max was saying, nodding to Randy. "Max Angeli," he said shortly, shaking hands with the other man. "And this is C.J. Kerry."

"We've met," C.J. noted, making an exasperated face at Randy before she favored Cari with a slight smile. "So nice to meet you, date stealer," she said, making it obvious she was joking, but letting the edge to her tone shine through all the same. "I'm glad we've got things straightened out at last."

Flustered, Cari wasn't sure what she said in return. Before she knew what was happening, Max was sliding in to sit beside her in the well-padded booth.

"Listen, Cari, I need some advice," he said, looking serious. "Do you mind?"

"Oh." Cari knew this had to be about the baby. "No, of course not." She turned toward him feeling a bit anxious.

"Hey," C.J. complained, still standing in the aisle, one hand on her hip. With her flaming hair and the tiny shimmering dress that just barely covered up her generous assets, she had heads turning all over the restaurant.

"You can sit down, too," Max told her in an offhanded manner. He nodded toward the seat beside Randy, who grinned and moved over eagerly, his eyes shining.

"Come on," Randy said to C.J., noting her outraged face. "I'm not so bad."

"Hah," she harrumphed, flouncing the ruffles of her glittering skirt, but she joined him willingly enough.

Max ignored her and leaned toward Cari. He was back in his Italian silk suit with the white shirt open at the throat, looking very sleek and continental. He'd shaved, which was a shame, really. But he still looked lethally sexy.

"The nanny was trying to get him to drink his evening bottle just before I left," he began. "He wouldn't touch it, wouldn't even let it into his mouth."

Cari frowned, growing a bit concerned. "Was he crying?"

He hesitated. "Not really. Just sort of whimpering." He thought for a minute. "But he did cry a lot earlier in the afternoon. It was enough to set your teeth on edge."

"And you're sure he wasn't in pain?"

Max shook his head, looking tortured. "You know, that's really hard to say. Just looking at him, I would say no. I didn't see any sign of that. But it's kind of hard to be sure when you don't speak their language, you know?"

Cari bit her lip, nodding. She could remember many long nights walking the floor with Michelle, wondering whether or not to call the doctor. Barring overt signs of illness, injury or distress, that was always a wrenching decision, especially at two in the morning.

"So here's what I want to know," he went on, gazing hard into her eyes, taking up all her attention. "Should I fire the nanny?"

Cari stared back at him. A part of her knew he had no business asking her to give him this sort of advice. What was she to him? She had no responsibility, no ties to this child. Why would he ask her?

But another part wanted to make sure baby Jamie was safe just as much as he did. The thought of a baby left to the winds of chance horrified her any time she came across such a situation. Babies needed protection at all times.

"Do you have someone else you can call?" she asked.

He shook his head, his eyes never leaving hers.

She could see how much this was bothering him, and it completely surprised her. She never would have pegged him for the sensitive type. That was the good thing. But he sure couldn't seem to handle a crying child. That was the bad thing—a warning flag to her. Brian had been totally intolerant of baby noises. That had been exactly what had triggered what had happened the nightmare night of the accident.

But she couldn't think about that. This was completely different. Max wasn't Brian. And listening to babies cry could be very frustrating, especially when you didn't really know the child. But babies did cry. Sometimes it was nothing more than being unfamiliar with their new surroundings.

"Give it until morning," she suggested. "By then you'll have enough experience with the woman to know if you want her to stay or not."

He seemed to wince and looked away. It was obvious

he wanted to be told his instincts were right and he should fire the woman.

C.J. had been watching their exchange, her gaze going back and forth between them as though it were a Ping-Pong match. "So, let me get this straight. You two have a baby together?"

They both looked at her and cried in unison "No!"

"No, no, no," Max amplified, looking impatient with the interruption. "This is my brother's baby."

"Oh." C.J. looked surprised. "I didn't know Gino had a baby."

They stared at her.

"You knew Gino?" Max demanded.

"Sure." She smiled, looking pleased that the attention was back where—in her mind—it belonged. "I met him when he was here last year."

Max looked incredulous. "Gino was here? What for?"

She shrugged. "Pretty much the same thing you're here for," she noted, giving him a sly look. "He wanted to buy the ranch."

Max's head went back. This was news to him. He and his brother had been close in many ways, including the family real estate development business they had taken over from their father and ran together. Why would Gino have come to Texas without telling him? It didn't make a lot of sense. Unless he'd been as intent on doing something to make their mother happy as he was himself.

"You know that he recently died in a plane crash,

don't you?" he asked her, grimacing at the effort it took to talk casually about him when the pain was still so raw.

"Yes, I know, and I'm so sorry about that." She nodded her sympathy and actually looked as though she meant it. "He seemed like a great guy. Though I didn't care much for the woman he had with him."

"Sheila?" Max frowned.

"Yes, I think that was her name." C.J. made a face. "Shifty looking." Then her face changed as though she'd just remembered something. "Actually, funny thing. I heard from her the other day. She was on my answering machine. I didn't call her back. She said she was here in town, and I could tell she was going to be asking for money."

"You were probably right. She's been doing a lot of that lately." Max was staring at her hard, as though he was seeing something new in her, something that gave him pause. "So Gino couldn't talk you into selling," he said softly.

"Of course not." Her chin came up and her huge green eyes were glittering with resolve. "I'm not selling the ranch. Ever. It's my heritage. It's all I've got now that all my family is gone."

Max's dark eyes narrowed speculatively as he gazed at the woman, but the server arrived with the drinks before he could make a comment on what she'd said.

"We should go get ourselves a table, honey," C.J. said to him, raising an eyebrow for emphasis.

He looked around as though surprised to find they

weren't where they belonged. Then he decided to do something about it. "There's plenty of room at this table," he said. "Let's eat here."

"What?" the other three cried, staring at him.

"Is there a problem?" he asked, looking from person to person. There was no sense of give to his attitude, and the others were the ones to back down. One by one, each reluctantly shook his or her head, as he looked at them.

"No. Of course not."

"Well, then." He shrugged and looked at the server. "I'll have a Scotch, neat. And you?" He nodded toward C.J.

C.J. ordered, but Cari wasn't listening any longer. This evening was turning out almost as surreal as the last one had been. If only Mara had left well enough alone in the first place, she would be home right now with some soft music playing and a nice novel in her hand. If only!

As they ordered their meals and the first course came, Randy and C.J. seemed to be doing all the talking. They were bantering back and forth about things they'd done the night before and what it was like to have been dumped by their respective blind dates. They'd started out using it as a way to tweak Cari and Max, but as things went along, they seemed to be wrapped up in their own little joke, leaving the other two behind.

Not that she cared. Her attention was full of the man beside her and didn't have much room left for the other two at the table. Max was quiet, almost morose, as though he were pondering life and all its unpleasant pitfalls and annoying blind alleys, and feeling glum about the prospects for happiness in general.

And Cari felt some sympathy for that point of view. She was wondering how she could have chosen the right path at her mythical fork in the road and yet have wound up on the wrong leg of the journey, anyway. Surely there had to be a shortcut to sanity somewhere. She had to get back where she belonged. But every minute she spent in the company of this man only made things worse. Just sitting here in his presence seemed to solidify the extraordinary attraction she felt for him. There was no getting around it—he was hot!

And that was bad. Sexual attraction was an illusion that clouded the mind and made you do stupid things. She had to guard against it. Experience suggested she was susceptible to the influence of strong men, and she had to fight the temptation to succumb. It wasn't easy.

Every time his gaze accidentally met hers, every time his hand brushed her arm, every time he spoke and his voice seemed to resonate in her soul, all she could think about was the way that full, luscious mouth had felt on hers the night before. This was making her nervous. It took all her control to keep from shaking like a leaf.

At one point, she almost knocked over her wineglass and Max reached out to steady it for her, leaning in close to do it. His crisp, clean scent filled her head, and the sense of his pure masculinity swept over her like a tantalizing breeze.

"Stop it," she thought to herself, feeling a bit desperate. "Just stop doing that."

"Stop what?" he murmured as he drew back, looking at her in that heavy-lidded way that caught at the breath in her throat. "I'm not doing anything."

She stared at him, aghast. She'd only thought the words, surely. How could he have heard her? Had she actually said them aloud—or was she going crazy?

Okay, the votes were in. She was going crazy. Here she was, sitting beside a man who could never be for her, but could ruin her for all the other men in the world if she didn't watch her step. And what was she doing? Gulping down wine like it was high noon in the Gobi Desert.

Smart, Cari, my dear. Very smart.

Ooops. She looked up quickly, wondering if she'd said *that* aloud, too. But no one was paying any attention to her. What a relief. Putting her head down, she began to eat automatically. If she cleaned her plate, maybe she would be allowed to go home to that book.

Max was pushing the food around on his own plate. Eating was the last thing he felt like doing right now. His usual calm sense of confidence seemed to be fraying a bit around the edges tonight. Things weren't going his way. In the first place he was disturbed by C.J.'s attitude. Her bony little feet seemed to be encased in concrete, where holding on to the ranch was concerned. He could tell she thought she was going to scam him. She was just as set on her path as he was on his. He hated to think what that might mean for his long-term prospects of success.

But most of all, he was worried about the baby. What did he know from babies? He was desperately determined to do right by this one, but doubts kept nagging at him. He looked at his watch, wondering how soon he would be able to bid C.J. adieu so he could go back and make sure Mrs. Turner hadn't fallen asleep in the comfortable chair, leaving Jamie to cry his little heart out.

He looked at Cari, wishing she'd agreed to let him hire her for the job. Instinctively he knew he could trust her with the baby. He'd already seen her in action on that score.

She was acting very jumpy at the moment. Every time he caught her eye, she looked away quickly, as though she was afraid he'd think she liked him or something. Hell, *he* didn't like anybody. He had a couple of things to accomplish and "liking" had nothing to do with either thing.

Still, he had to admit he was drawn to her in a way that was unusual for him. He kept thinking about her, even when she was across town working in that funny little café full of cowboys. But mostly he was sure that was because she could be the answer to some of his biggest problems if she would only agree to help him. Though maybe there was a bit more to it than that. After all, he was human, and

for a woman who was not really his type, she looked darn
appealing tonight. Her little blue dress revealed some
very delectable skin that hadn't seen the light of day for
a while. But he wasn't supposed to be thinking about that.

"You know what?" she said suddenly, leaning toward
him and speaking quietly. "I've been thinking. If you
want, I could come by after dinner, just for a few minutes, and sort of scope out the situation. See what I
think of the nanny."

He stared at her. She was not only the most beautiful woman in the world, how was it he had never noticed
that shiny gold halo that hovered over her head? Or
those big gorgeous white wings fluttering off her back?
There was actually a lump in his throat. He didn't trust
his voice, and he nodded.

"Great," he managed at last, though it sounded
creaky. "Great."

She must have seen the abject relief and gratitude in
his eyes, because she looked startled and drew back as
though she was already regretting the offer.

"Excuse me," she said, gathering her little purse and
gesturing toward the way out. "I'm going to go powder
my nose."

"Me too," said C.J., sliding out right behind her.

Max rose and let her out, amazed at the peace she'd
given him with her suggestion to come by and take a
look at the nanny. He hated having things hanging over
his head this way. When there was a problem, he was
used to dealing with it so it would go away. This nanny

thing had been like a bad toothache gnawing away at him all day. And now he was going to be able to do something about it. Thanks to Cari.

Sliding back into his seat, he smiled at Randy. "Wonderful woman, isn't she?" he noted.

And Randy nodded. "Sure is," he said, though he wasn't really sure which woman they were talking about.

Cari had groaned inside the moment she realized C.J. was really going to accompany her to the restroom, but she didn't let it show. The last thing she wanted was company. That was exactly what she was trying to get away from. Nevertheless, C.J. came along, chatting incessantly as they moved through the dining room and headed into the ladies' lounge. Inside, huge mirrors lined the walls with low vanities and comfortable chairs facing them. Cari sank into one of the chairs and pretended to freshen her makeup. C.J. chattered on.

"That Randy is so funny," she said, draping herself across the neighboring chair and fluffing her brilliant hair as she watched herself in the mirror. "He keeps me in stitches."

"He said pretty much the same about you."

"Did he? Aw, that's sweet."

Cari looked into C.J.'s face. She'd already realized the woman was smarter than she seemed at first glance. So what was her purpose here? Surely she'd come along for a reason.

"So what do you do, C.J.?" Max had said something

about a ranch, but the woman didn't look like a working rancher. "For a living, I mean."

"Well, that's a question, isn't it?" C.J. flipped her hair back behind her ears and made a face at herself in the mirror. "I tried college. Didn't like it. Did some modeling. That was sooo boring. Worked for a while in my friend's boutique, but that didn't pay enough to keep a parakeet alive."

Turning, she leaned toward Cari, who tensed, pretty sure the point was about to be made.

"So I looked around to see what I could do to keep myself in high-fashion lingerie and late-model luxury cars, and I finally realized marrying a rich man seemed to be the best match for my talents."

"Oh." Cari almost laughed aloud. What incredible nerve the woman had! "It's a blessing to know yourself, I guess."

"It sure is. Saves a lot of unnecessary heartache." She slicked on some lipstick, pursed her lips, and then looked straight at Cari. "Which reminds me. Just to let you know. I consider Max my territory. I went and planted my little flag in his big ole chest and I mean to bring him in alive."

Cari choked, amazed at the woman's candor. She looked at her in wonder. "Does he have anything to say about this?"

C.J. shrugged, smiling smugly. "Not much. You see, I've got an ace in the hole."

"Do you?"

"Sure enough." She nodded. "It's no secret that his

mama is crazy to get her hands on my ranch. She's got sentimental ties and all that. I let it be known that I love that place like an armadillo loves the yellow line down the center of the road." She snapped her fingers. "The results are as good as in the bag."

Cari shook her head, appalled and amused at the same time. "Why are you telling me this? Aren't you afraid I might tell Max?"

"Tell him." She shrugged good-naturedly. "He knows. Facts are facts. I've got something he wants and there's just one way he's going to get it. We both know the score. I'm just warning you not to try poaching in my paddock."

Cari had no intention of doing any such thing, but the woman's attitude certainly rubbed her the wrong way and she was tempted to pretend she had her own designs on Max. It was on the tip of her tongue to blurt out, "Make me!" but that would be childish. Satisfying, but childish. So instead, she rose from her chair with dignity and turned to go.

"Well, we'll see what happens," she said calmly.

"You got that right," C.J. said, coming right behind her. "May the toughest gal win."

Cari turned on a dime and stared at C.J. "Wait a minute. I'm not trying to win. I don't want Max."

"Don't you?" C.J.'s smile reminded Cari of a Disney crocodile. "That's okay, then. I assume you'll be keeping your cute little hands off my man. So all will be well." She shrugged extravagantly. "Forget I said anything."

Cari was still fuming when they got back to the booth. Max rose to let her in and she threw him a dirty look as she squeezed past him, even though she knew he had no idea what C.J. had been saying. By the time she'd calmed down and was listening to the conversation again, they were back talking about nannies.

"You better watch out," Randy was saying. "You know, they've been catching some of these nannies on those Nannycams, just throwing the babies around like a bushel of old sticks."

Cari's heart leaped into her throat, and when she noticed Max's vaguely grim look, she said quickly, "That's very rare, as I understand it."

"Sure. But it happens."

"Well, it won't happen to Jamie. The nanny Max has hired comes very highly recommended. She may not be the right fit for what Max needs, but she certainly wouldn't do something like that."

The conversation moved on with C.J. and Randy talking animatedly, but Cari was staring down at her plate. All she could think about was Jamie being thrown about like a discarded package. Echoes of what had happened to her own baby that terrible night. That little neck. That little head. Suddenly she felt sick to her stomach. Glancing over, she saw that Max wasn't looking tip-top, either.

Their eyes met and she could read thoughts very similar to hers written plainly on his face.

"Maybe we should just go check right now," she said softly.

He nodded. Reaching under the table, she covered his hand with hers and gave it a quick squeeze before she could stop herself. Drawing back, she wondered if he would understand that the gesture of comfort had been about Jamie and nothing else. Maybe not. But she didn't have time or energy to repair that blunder right now. Later she might have to explain. She turned her attention back to the others.

"Listen, folks," Max began. "New game plan. I'm going back to my place so I can check out the nanny. Cari has agreed to come along and help me. Are the two of you with us?"

Cari had to admit the flash of fire in C.J.'s eyes as they met hers made the whole thing worth it. But she also knew there was no way the woman was going to let her go off to Max's unescorted. With a sigh, she resigned herself to a long, long evening.

CHAPTER SIX

THEY could hear Jamie crying the moment they stepped off the elevator. Max's face turned to stone and he strode quickly to the door of the suite, using his card to unlock it. He disappeared inside. By the time the rest of them made it down the hallway and entered the room, Mrs. Turner was already packing up her things and preparing to leave.

"Well, I never," she was saying indignantly.

"Just go, Mrs. Turner." Max was having a hard time remaining calm. "I'll contact the agency and have the rest of your things sent over in the morning."

Cari didn't waste any time with the woman. She went straight into the bedroom and crossed the floor to the crib. There was Jamie, crying his heart out. Reaching down, she picked him up.

"There, there," she crooned lovingly as she pressed him to her chest. "It's all right, darling. It's all right."

Jamie's sobs turned into a long, heartfelt sigh, interrupted by a very loud hiccup. And then he quieted.

There was a sense of relief in his last little whimpers, as though he recognized her and was saying, "Finally! Where've you been, anyway?"

She cuddled him close, breathed in his baby smell and felt a little bubble of joy burst in her heart. She'd missed this all day long. It made her wince to think she could have been here, could have been taking care of this child. She mustn't let all her personal rules and fears keep her away. For once, she had to follow her heart, no matter where it led her. At least for now.

"Oh, you little sweetheart," she whispered against the dark hair on his baby head. "How can you be so sweet?"

"Well, she's gone."

Cari looked up to see Max standing in the doorway. She tried to read his eyes. There was something she had to know. Jamie's crying had sent him over the edge. That had happened right there in front of them all. There was no denying it. But had it been because of his empathy for the baby? Or was it because he didn't think the nanny was doing a good job—and he couldn't tolerate shoddy work from those who worked for him? Or had it been her nightmare fear—was it because of anger at the noise? That was a question that would haunt her until she knew the answer for sure.

She could see he was upset, though he tried to hide it behind his stoic, emotionless mask. But did he feel for the baby? Or was he annoyed with him? He hadn't made a move to come to him, to comfort him or touch him in any way. What did that mean? She held Jamie closer and knew she couldn't just walk away this time.

"All well and good," C.J. was saying as she came into the room behind him. "But what happens now? You're just going to have to hire another one."

"I'll get a better one," he said stoutly. "I think I'm getting a better handle on this job now. I'll know what to ask in the interview. I'll ask questions about child care methods and philosophy. I'll set up some scenarios and ask the woman how she would deal with each situation." He turned to C.J. and Randy. "Did you see her? Sitting there eating a cupcake and yakking away on the phone while the baby was crying. That wasn't child care, that was child neglect."

C.J. shrugged as though it was all the same to her. Randy nodded sympathetically. And Max turned to Cari to see what she thought. But she wasn't giving anything away. Not yet.

He came closer and looked down at the child, who was now gurgling happily.

"Listen, you're going to have to teach me how to hold him," he said, favoring her with a slight smile. "I'm not up on this stuff."

She nodded. "All right," she responded, heartened that he wanted to learn, but still wary.

"Good. And you can fill me in on anything else I should know before I hire another nanny."

She nodded again, meeting his gaze and searching his eyes. They were clear and intelligent. She couldn't detect any lingering anger or uneasiness. In fact, he looked relieved. That was good. But could she trust it?

"And right from the start," Max went on, "I'm going to have one of those Nannycam cameras installed." He nodded, looking around at the corners of the room as though planning where the camera would be. "That will help."

Cari took a deep breath. She was about to take a step here, and she knew it was going to put her in emotional jeopardy. But she'd come this far and she couldn't back down now.

"Forget the cameras," she said, then pressed her lips together resolutely.

Max swung around and stared at her. "Why would I do that?"

Lifting her chin, she gazed steadily into his eyes. "I'm staying. I'll take care of him. At least for now."

"What?" He frowned as though he didn't trust her motives.

She felt a quick twinge of exasperation. He'd been trying to talk her into this all day, and now that she'd agreed, he looked as if he'd rather go back to talking instead.

"I can't disrupt your life that way," he said, shaking his head and frowning at her, his expression wary.

She threw him a look. "I think you already have."

"Wait a minute," C.J. was saying, unable to believe what she was hearing. "You can't do that."

Cari looked at her over Jamie's little head. "Sure I

can," she said calmly. "Why don't you stay, too, C.J.? I could use the help." She pretended to smile and made her eyes big and innocent. "We could share a bed, you and I."

C.J. recoiled. "Are you kidding?" She shuddered. "Anyway, babies give me the willies."

Cari turned away. They could go on bickering about anything they chose, she'd made her own choice. She was staying with the baby. There wasn't anyone else looking out for him.

Max seemed to have his best interests at heart, but she couldn't be sure. Some men couldn't be with babies. She knew that from experience. Someone had to be Jamie's champion in the world. At least until his mother showed up, she would be the one.

An hour later they were alone. Randy took a very annoyed C.J. back to her car. Cari taught Max how to hold the baby. He was quick to pick up the subtle nuances. All in all, she thought he was a pretty good student of on-the-fly child care.

"I wouldn't say you're a natural exactly," she teased him as he awkwardly patted the baby he held against his shoulder. "But you'll do for now."

Jamie chose that moment to spit up. Luckily, Cari had taught Max to throw a clean burp pad over his shoulder before picking up the baby, so his silk shirt was protected. Still, the sound of the very loud burp made Max cringe and made Cari laugh.

"We'll move on to bottle feeding tomorrow," she warned him. "Think you're up for it?"

"Why not?"

They put the baby down in his crib. Cari cooed to him as his big brown eyes drifted shut. Max watched her more than he watched the baby. There was something about her that just made him feel happy to be around. Very odd.

"Cari." He took her hands in his and gazed deeply into her eyes. "I am so grateful to you for doing this. I can't tell you how much I appreciate it."

It was true. He'd been going nuts ever since he'd brought Mrs. Turner in and she'd begun her tyrannical reign over his hotel suite. Well, he supposed it hadn't been that bad, really. But it had been bad enough. The dilemma had been whether to trust her or not when everything she did just seemed wrong to him.

With Cari it was different. Maybe they were on the same wavelength. Or maybe he just liked her better. It didn't matter. What did matter was that he was calm inside. There was no longer a battle raging between his heart and his head.

"Don't think of it as me doing something for you," she said pertly. "I'm doing this for Jamie."

He only half believed her. He knew there was a provocative buzz between the two of them. She couldn't deny it, though he could see she wanted to. As though to remind her, he smiled and dropped a quick kiss on her lips.

She drew back, eyes widening. "No, Max," she said quickly. "I didn't stay for that. Honestly, I didn't."

"I know. I'm sorry." But he didn't sound very convincing, even to himself.

She turned and began putting away toys and supplies. He watched her for a moment, then asked, "So tell me, Cari, where did you learn so much about babies?"

To his surprise she froze for a moment, then turned slowly and looked at him with huge, shadowed eyes.

"I had one," she said softly.

That surprised him. "You have a baby?"

She shook her head. "Not anymore. She died."

His breath caught in his throat in a way it had never done before. Shock knifed through him and he felt pain for her.

"Oh, Cari," he began, moving toward her.

She went ramrod stiff, holding him at bay. "I was married, you know," she said quickly.

He hesitated, fighting the urge to take her in his arms for comfort. "No, I didn't."

"My husband and my baby both died in a car accident. It was two years ago."

"Cari, I'm so sorry."

She shook her head, not quite meeting his gaze. "Now you know. Okay. I'd rather not talk about it."

"Of course."

He watched as she gathered things into piles to go through in the morning. Knowing that she'd been married, knowing about the tragedy in her past, answered a lot of questions for him. He'd known there was something disturbing her. Now he thought he knew what that was. No wonder she seemed to hold the world at arm's length. To have lost her baby and her husband at such a young age—horrible.

He wanted to hold her close and make it all go away, but he knew she would reject that. He would have to bide his time. Maybe once she knew him better, she would trust him. Oddly enough, he wanted that badly. In fact, he ached to do something for her—anything, and he wasn't sure why he felt that way.

Oh, he knew the mechanics. She'd had tragedy. He cared about her and wanted to do something to help her get over the agony of it. But why did he seem to have this deep, unfamiliar need to do that? He didn't remember ever having it before, not with anyone outside of his immediate family. Very strange.

Tito came in from visiting relatives in a local suburb. He was surprised to see Cari there, but welcoming enough. Still, he went off to his own room pretty quickly. And Cari knew it was time to get her sleeping arrangements settled.

She didn't want to stay in the room Mrs. Turner had used. The nanny's bags were still scattered across the floor, and her clothes were in the closet and dresser. So Max ordered up a rollaway and set up the bed in the baby's room. That was for the best. She wanted Jamie to have the feeling someone was always there for him. No gaps. No more being left to cry his heart out on his own.

"I actually understand the theory behind what Mrs. Turner meant to do with him," she told Max as they were arranging the room. "It doesn't do to let babies think they can manipulate you all the time. But Jamie's case is special. He's missing his mom and he needs extra love to make him feel secure right now, not discipline."

"I think you're probably right," Max told her, talking softly so as not to wake the baby. "I sure feel more comfortable with your methods than I did with the nanny's."

"Good." She smiled at him. Everything he said was reassuring her. Still, she knew the best of intentions could evaporate when one was under stress. She wanted to be there in case she was needed as a buffer. There was no substitute for hands-on child care.

"I'm going to need something to sleep in," she pointed out, looking down at the blue cocktail dress. It gave her a start to notice how low the neckline was. She'd forgotten. Her cheeks felt hot. Looking up, she saw that Max had been watching and was reading her mind. The awareness between them almost made her gasp. She turned away quickly and didn't look at him again until he left the room and came back with a large T-shirt for her to use as a nightgown.

He began to talk about random things and she realized he was trying to put her at ease again. She appreciated that, but she didn't feel comfortable. Despite the presence of Tito in the room on the other side of the suite, they were basically alone together. That made him a threat—to her peace of mind at least. He was too potent a force to ignore.

At one point, he made a comment about C.J. and she couldn't help but give her own take on things.

"She means to marry you, you know," she said, looking down into the crib at Jamie as he slept.

He didn't flinch. Coming up beside her, he smiled down at the drowsy baby. "Yes," he said casually. "I was hoping it wouldn't come to that. But I'm afraid you're right."

She turned to look at him in exasperation. "How can you be so calm about it? You hardly know her. I mean, you thought I was her last night."

"I wish I'd been right," he said dryly, and she gasped, but he was smiling. He turned and gazed at her as though her naiveté amused him. "This is not a love match, Cari. If there is anything to it, it's more like a business deal."

"That's exactly what she told me," she noted, nodding. "You marry her, your mother gets the ranch. Isn't that the way it goes?"

"Pretty much."

She shook her head. "It sounds crazy to me."

"Life can be crazy sometimes," he said vaguely, waving her objection away. "But it has its own special logic. People get married for all sorts of reasons. To do it as part of an exchange of goods is one of the most ancient methods in every culture."

"It seems way too medieval."

"Really? What will you marry again for, Cari? Love?"

His voice rang with sarcasm at the word, as though

he didn't believe in it. That put her back up a bit, and yet she couldn't really argue with him when she was going to deny the need to love in her own right.

"I won't marry again at all," she said instead. "I don't need a man in my life."

He stared at her for a moment, then threw back his head and laughed out loud. "You're priceless, Cari," he said. "But this is the way it is. I've been dating women for over fifteen years now. I've yet to find one I desperately want to spend the rest of my life with. Evidence suggests she's not going to come breaking out of the woodwork anytime soon. So why not use a marriage to get what I want?"

She snorted. His cynicism appalled her. "The question is, why do you want it?"

"To save my mother's life."

That shut her up. She couldn't help but feel it was a bit melodramatic. She supposed that was the Italian in him. But it left her speechless nonetheless. After all, what would she be willing to do for the people she loved best?

"Not that," she whispered to herself as he turned and left the room.

She watched him go, then followed him out into the living room, ready to ask him more about this, but he sandbagged her with a question of his own.

"So what did you think of your blind date?" he asked, sinking into the sleek yet comfortable couch.

"Who? Randy?" She flopped down into a chair

across from where he was sitting. Her chin rose. "Obviously, he's perfect for me," she said with only a tiny touch of sarcasm.

He caught her nuance. "Is he?" Amusement danced in his dark eyes.

"Of course." She shrugged. "Hand picked, in fact, by my best friend, Mara. And she was right. Can't you tell?"

He allowed himself a halfhearted grin. "Oh, yeah. Nice guy. Funny guy. I enjoyed him."

"Me, too." She punched a pillow. "He's exactly the sort of man I need."

"Ya think?"

"Yes." She faced him frankly. "He's very calm and very…" She drew in a long, deep breath. "Very ordinary."

"Ordinary." He frowned thoughtfully, then raised an eyebrow. He'd never thought of that quality as an attribute. "Is that a plus?"

She nodded. "I'm ordinary. What's wrong with ordinary?"

He gave her a look. Maybe the word didn't mean just what he thought it did. "Did I say anything was wrong with ordinary?"

"Ordinary can be okay," she said a bit defensively. "I come from ordinary people. My father was an accountant, my mother worked in a bank."

"Do they live in Dallas?"

She shook her head. "No. My mother died of cancer and my father died of a broken heart."

"Ah." He nodded. He understood that sort of thing.

"It's true you don't get the thrilling highs with ordinary," she went on. "But you don't get the bone-rattling lows, either." She winced, thinking of Brian. "Excitement can be scary when it goes bad," she added softly.

He noted the haunted look in her eyes as she spoke. There had been some scary excitement in her life, something that had gone badly. Of course, there were the deaths of her husband and child she'd told him about. Tragedies like that could have life-crippling effects on a person. But he had a feeling this was something more deeply rooted in the past, and maybe more specific to one person—for instance, her husband. What else could have made her so wary of a relationship?

It only made sense. When you lost a significant other who made you happy, you tended to be in a hurry to replicate that happiness as soon as the grieving period began to die down a bit. People with good relationships believed in good relationships. She was scared to connect. Something had gone wrong somewhere along the line.

He wanted to ask her about that, find out what was troubling her, but he held back. He didn't want to scare her off, and he knew she didn't want to talk about personal things. She had to be coaxed, cajoled and brought along casually. He would take his time.

"So what about me?" he said instead. "Would you call me an ordinary guy?"

"Hardly." Her sudden smile was like the sun coming

out from behind a cloud, fascinating him. "You're the sort mothers warn their daughters to stay away from, don't you think?"

"Me?" He was genuinely startled that she felt that way. Truth to tell, he didn't consider himself exactly ordinary, but he didn't relish the bad-boy role either. "So what's scary about me?"

"Nothing, I guess." She was still smiling that radiant smile. "You haven't scared me yet."

He noted the "yet."

"But you *are* a little larger than life," she added, just to be clear.

He frowned, not sure he was going to like this. "In what way?"

"Let's just put it this way—you're a little too exciting. Too good-looking. Too powerful. Too adventurous. Shall I go on?"

"No. That's plenty." His frown deepened. "And not really fair."

"Fair has nothing to do with it," she told him firmly. "Do you think it's fair that I'm definitely ordinary? I can't help it. I was born this way. And naturally, if I'm going to have a relationship again, I need an ordinary man."

There it was, the point this whole conversation seemed to be leading up to. She was giving him a message.

"Like Randy," he said softly.

She nodded, her eyes huge in the gloomy light. "Yes."

He gave her an incredulous look. Randy was all well

and good, but he wasn't right for Cari. She needed someone…well, someone more like Max himself. Someone with a little style and energy.

"You need excitement," he stated firmly.

She shook her head, challenging him with her bright gaze. "No. I need security."

He stared at her, mulling that over. What did she think she was, ready for retirement?

"Bull," he said at last. Rising from the couch, he erased the distance between them, reached out and took her hand and pulled her up to face him.

"What in hell makes you think you're ordinary?" he demanded, face-to-face. "You're careful. You're responsible. You're a good person. If you think that makes you ordinary, you have a higher definition of the term than I do." He looked deep into her eyes. "I think that makes you pretty special."

She was tingling. He made her tingle more and more lately. Was that a good thing? Probably not.

What if he was right? That was what scared her. The thing was, Randy was exactly the kind of man she had decided she could deal with, if the need came. Mara had said it best—Randy was perfect. But did her senses zing when he smiled at her? Did she feel faint when he touched her? Did her breathing stall when he whispered near her ear? Did she tingle?

Hardly. Things never worked out that way, did they?

"I think it's time to go to bed," she said, pulling away from him and backing toward the nursery.

"Alone?" he said, pretending a plaintive tone, but obviously just teasing.

"Alone." She smiled one last time, then turned, went into the nursery and closed the door.

CHAPTER SEVEN

IF MAX had been one to fantasize what mornings with a wife and child would be like, this would have been a part of that dream. He walked into the nursery with two mugs of coffee and there was Cari, standing in the sunlight streaming in through the window with a baby in her arms, singing a lullaby. She wore his big T-shirt and nothing else, and her bare legs looked golden and gorgeous in the morning light. She turned to greet him, her hair wild around her face, and she smiled that smile that could knock him dead, beaming happiness and welcome.

He stopped in his tracks and stared at her. *"Bella,"* he said softly. *"Bellissima."*

"I didn't think you'd be up this early," she said. Her gaze traveled appreciatively over him in a way that made his pulse quicken. He'd put on a pair of tight jeans and a shirt he hadn't buttoned yet out of expediency, but if she would like what she saw as much as she seemed to, he would do it more often.

"I brought coffee," he said.

"I see that," she replied.

"Here." He set the mugs down on the dresser and turned to her. "Let me hold him."

Her eyes widened. "You really want to?"

He nodded. "If all goes well, I'm planning to raise this child," he said simply. "I want to do it right."

"If all goes well," she echoed thoughtfully as she handed Jamie to him. "In other words, if Sheila lets you take him." And why would a mother do that without putting up a very fierce fight? Well, she had to admit, this mother didn't seem to be quite as interested in being a mother as one would hope. Max might very well be able to negotiate something with her for enough money. But that was only a part of the problem.

She frowned, then asked a question she knew would be unpopular. "What if the DNA comes back negative, Max? What if there is no biologic connection to your brother? What then?"

He shrugged dismissively, smiling down at Jamie all the while. "I don't think that will happen."

"But don't you think you ought to be prepared just in case? What do you plan to do with this baby if he isn't Gino's?"

His gaze rose and met hers. "I've already talked to a lawyer. They're setting up legal strategies for when the DNA results comes in. We'll play it by ear."

Cari felt chilled. "If Sheila isn't found and Jamie isn't Gino's, will you just go off and leave him?"

His face hardened. "Cari, I told you, I don't think that is something we will have to face. Drop it."

He was right. She had to drop it. If she didn't, she would be riling herself up over something she couldn't do anything about. It was best to let it be for now. Taking a deep breath, she steadied herself and tried to move on.

But the prospect of seeing Jamie abandoned wouldn't fade from her mind. She knew she couldn't let that happen. If it came to that, she would do something. It only bothered her that Max couldn't make that commitment himself right now. And that made her think she'd been right to come to stay with them. Someone had to protect the baby.

They played with Jamie for another ten minutes and then his eyelids began to droop. Max laid him down gently in the crib and Cari pulled his little blanket up over him.

"Isn't he adorable?" she said, smiling down at the shocking head of dark hair.

"He's okay," Max said gruffly. "He'll do."

She smiled to herself. He was more soft on Jamie than he would admit. It wouldn't be long before he wouldn't be able to turn his back on this baby no matter what.

Looking up, she found him watching her, and his intention was clear as a bell.

"Max," she said warningly, taking a step backward. He was looking very seductive in a very Italian way, and she was feeling particularly susceptible to Italians this morning. Danger!

Reaching out, he put a finger under her chin and

tilted her face up. "I'm sorry Cari, but you're too beautiful to resist this morning. I have to kiss you."

"Oh, Max, no."

"Just a simple good-morning kiss. Nothing more."

"Max…"

Somehow his name turned into a sigh, and then she was parting her lips to accept his mouth on hers. She shouldn't do this. She'd warned herself from the start not to let this happen. But now that he was here, so close, so male, so hard and insistent, she felt so soft, so female, so ready to mold herself to whatever his passion might suggest. His mouth was hot, his tongue provocative, and she sensed her own needs beginning to waken from a long, long slumber.

His shirt was still open and she ran her hands over his muscular chest, trembling as she felt the pounding of his heart beneath her fingers. He groaned, pulling her closer, and she melted like wax against his tall, hard frame. There was only the thin fabric of the T-shirt between them. He wanted her with a force that stunned him. This was something on a different level than he usually felt. This was new. This was sweeter and more overpowering than he was used to.

He sighed against her neck, murmuring her name as he dropped kisses and let his tongue caress her. She gasped as the heat from his body flooded her with sensation. She could sense his desire quickening and that gave her a taste of power she'd never known before. He was reacting to what her body did to him. That took her breath away.

She knew it was time to put a stop to this, but she couldn't quite muster the strength to do it yet. She was struggling to surface from a sea of pleasure, struggling to push her head back above water and breathe real air instead of this enchanted substance that felt so intoxicating, but was so dangerous. The truth was, she didn't want to stop.

And then there was a loud knocking at the door of the suite.

"Hey, y'all, here we are."

The voice was C.J.'s. The groan was Max's. He dropped his face into the curve of her neck and swore softly as he dropped a string of kisses on her skin.

"What time is it?" Cari murmured groggily as he began to pull back from her.

"Too early for visitors," Max grumbled.

But he unwrapped his arms from around her reluctantly and went to the door anyway, letting in C.J. and Randy. Cari watched him go, feeling cold all of a sudden. Max's simple morning kiss had proven to be pretty darn special. She could grow to like this. In fact, she might get addicted if she didn't watch out.

She pulled her arms in and hugged them close. But no matter how hard she held herself, she knew she would never come close to duplicating the magic of Max's embrace.

"We brought doughnuts," C.J. cried, waving the bag around as she entered the living room.

Cari slipped her fake fur shrug over the T-shirt and

looked at herself in the mirror. She looked ridiculous, but she didn't have much choice. It was either this or wrap herself in a bed sheet. So she came out, head held high and smiling.

And then she saw the doughnuts. Her downfall.

"Wow," she said as C.J. spilled them out onto a plate. "Those look great."

"Don't they? We got them at a bakery Randy deals with."

C.J. looked at her sharply, and she knew she was looking for signs of hanky-panky. The signs might very well be there. Cari was still reeling from Max's kisses and she didn't really care who knew it. C.J.'s gaze raked over the giant-size T-shirt with disdain, but Cari met her gaze unblinkingly. Whatever C.J. thought, she wasn't going to show her any embarrassment. Let her deal with *that*.

C.J. pursed her lips, but seemed to accept that there was nothing she could do about anything between Max and Cari at the moment, so she let it go.

"Did you know our boy Randy has a catering business?" she said, giving him a quick smile that served to include him in the group.

Cari blinked, looking at the jovial man. "I thought you were a stockbroker."

"That's my day job." He grinned at her and snagged the biggest doughnut.

"He hates it," C.J. announced to the world at large. "That's why he started up this little ole catering business on the side. He loves setting up parties."

"No kidding." Cari wondered if Mara knew about that side of her husband's cousin. He looked more like a stock-broker than a caterer, but then, what did a caterer look like?

"Yup. I'm getting him some clients. I know people who give huge parties."

Cari was impressed. It seemed C.J. had her uses after all. "Wow. Lucky Randy."

She looked at him. He was grinning happily. It was evident he did feel like a lucky man today. Cari had to laugh inside. She might think Randy a perfect match for herself, but it was pretty obvious he had other plans. C.J. looked just right to him. Poor guy.

But then, how was Randy any more of an object of pity than she was herself? She sighed, feeling ordinary, and turned to the kitchenette to make coffee for the guests.

They were sitting around the table sipping coffee and munching on delicious donuts when C.J. dropped her bombshell.

"Hey, I talked to your mama this morning, Max."

His head rose sharply and he stared at her in horror. "You did what?"

"I called her. Don't worry, I paid attention to the time difference. She sure is nice. I just love her." She darted a particularly smug look Cari's way. "We had a great talk and we put our heads together and figured out a few ideas for presents you could get her before you go back to Venice. So I'm takin' you shopping, you lucky boy. I know all the best department stores in Dallas and I'm going to introduce you to them, too. We'll have a great time."

"What?" Max sounded like a drowning man.

"Oh, come on, you old meanie," C.J. said, slapping him playfully on the shoulder. "You want to make your mama happy, don't you?"

He looked to Cari for help, but she shrugged. "I'm going to be taking care of Jamie all day," she said serenely. "He needs a bath and then I'm going to take him out in his stroller."

"You'll probably need some help," Max said hopefully.

"Who, me? I don't think so." She favored him with a devilish grin. "You'd better go with C.J. and Randy. They've obviously got their hearts set on making you come out to play."

"I'm only going," Max told her a few minutes later as he finished dressing and prepared to meet the other two in the lobby, "so that I can get a chance to work on C.J. about selling the ranch. I've got a new angle I'm going to try on her."

"Why not just marry the woman and be done with it?" she teased. "I thought this was just a business deal."

He turned to look at her. "The more time I spend with her the more I realize business like that is a perilous game," he told her. "But you're right. I may have to marry her. I'm just going to do everything I can think of to avoid that fate." He looked back at her seriously as he started out the door. "But bottom line, I've got to get control of that ranch."

Her smile evaporated as the door closed. She hadn't

discerned one little bit of give in C.J.'s position, but maybe Max could find something. She certainly hoped so—for his sake.

Cari called the Copper Penny later in the morning to let them know she was going to take a few days off. She felt guilty leaving them in the lurch, but this was an emergency, and she had some time off she could use. Tito drove her home to pack up some clothes, and on the way back, they stopped at a baby store. Max had given her a credit card and told her to get what she thought they needed. It was a virtual baby wonderland and she ordered an outlandish amount of baby equipment to be delivered to the hotel.

That put her in a great mood. Shopping trips often seemed to have that effect—and something told her she was having a lot more fun than Max was right now.

Taking care of Jamie was a breeze. He was such a sweetheart, so responsive and free with his baby smiles and gurgles, that being with him was a joy. And dressing him in his cute new outfits was fun, too. She was glad he was a boy and about a month older than Michelle had been, so the comparisons and memories, though they did come up and did bring a wave of sadness, didn't sting the way they might have.

The situation that worried her most right now was the status of this baby. What was going to happen if the DNA result was negative? If Sheila appeared and had a good explanation for where she'd been, she supposed

Jamie would go back to his mother and the rest of them would go on with their lives. But what if Sheila was on drugs or something else that made her impossible as a mother to this little angel? That would present its own problems. But there was no point thinking about that. Sheila claimed this was Gino's baby and there was, so far, no reason to doubt her.

So what if Sheila didn't return and the test did come back with the result Max was looking for? What would happen then? It was perfectly obvious. Max would pack Jamie up and take off for Venice. She would lose again. Another heartbreak.

No, now she was letting her emotions run rampant. She wasn't that attached to this child and she wouldn't let herself be. She was a caretaker, nothing more.

And she wasn't going to fall in love—with either one of them.

It was midafternoon and Max wasn't back yet. Jamie was napping peacefully. Cari decided to take a shower. A few minutes later she was luxuriating in the multiple-spray waterfall of the fancy bathroom when she thought she heard something. She turned off the water, listening intently.

There it was. Jamie was crying. Wouldn't you know her timing wouldn't work out? Sighing, she stepped out of the shower and grabbed a towel and that was when she heard Max at the bathroom door.

"Cari, the baby's crying. Why is he crying?"

"Well, pick him up and see what he needs," she called back, toweling fast. She hurried to blot her hair and put on her robe. As she emerged from the bathroom, she could hear Jamie down the hall.

"I'm coming, I'm coming," she called, pulling the robe more tightly around her as she rushed down the hallway. In the nursery, Max was standing at the side of the crib looking down at Jamie. Cari pushed right past him and picked the baby up, cooing and rocking him as he slowly quieted down. Glancing up, she saw from the look on Max's face that he was not happy.

"Why was he crying?" he demanded.

This entire scene was putting a knot in her stomach. "Relax," she said shortly. "Babies do cry."

His frown was ferocious. "But if it was bad when the nanny let him cry…"

A scene flashed in her mind. It had been very late and she'd been frantically trying to heat a bottle and get it back to Michelle before Brian completely exploded.

"Can't you shut her up?" Brian had yelled from the bedroom. "I've gotta get some sleep. I've got to work in the morning, you know."

"Just a minute."

"Cari, if you don't shut that baby up I'm leaving. I can't live like this."

"Brian, just give me a minute…"

A crash came from the bedroom where Brian had thrown the lamp against the wall.

Cari blinked away the memory. She looked up into Max's face.

"You left him alone," he said accusingly. "Why did you leave him alone?"

Cari took a deep breath and gathered all her resources. "Max, listen to me carefully. He was asleep when I went to take a shower. He was only alone for a couple of minutes." She gazed at him earnestly. Surely he was mature enough to understand.

But maybe not. Maybe he was going to be like Brian. Her heart sank. If so, what would she do? She wouldn't dare leave the baby here with him, and yet how could she stay?

"Max, this is not a major issue. Babies do cry. You don't leave them alone to cry for hours, but now and then it's going to happen."

Fascinated, she watched him visibly begin to relax. He looked down at the baby and ran a hand through his hair, then looked up at her again. "I'm sorry," he said gruffly. "You're right, of course. It's just, I came in and heard him crying and didn't know where you'd gone."

A surge of relief that developed quickly into affection rolled through her. She wanted to touch him. She wanted to reach out and run her hand down the side of his face. Instead she challenged him.

"Here's a question for you. Why does the crying bother you so much?"

He stopped as though that was a new one he hadn't thought about before. "I guess it's because I'm afraid something is wrong and I won't know what to do about it," he admitted at last.

She smiled, feeling such relief. He wasn't like Brian. That was becoming clear.

"Good answer," she murmured. "So it's not just that the noise drives you crazy?"

"Well, I can't say I love the noise," he said. "But I don't think it's driving me crazy, exactly."

"Good."

She hugged him. It was spontaneous and it was one-handed and it was quick. In fact, it was over before he realized it was happening. And then she was gone again and leading the way out into the living room with Jamie in her arms.

"What all have you got there?" she cried, surveying the piles of packages in exclusive department store bags and boxes.

"You wouldn't believe it," he said, coming out behind her. "What I've got is presents. Presents for my mother. Presents for the servants at my mother's house in Venice. Presents for all the people who work for me." He shook his head, looking at her in bewilderment. "Why the hell do women love presents so much?"

She shrugged and grinned at him. "You're the one buying them."

He snarled just a little. "C.J. made me."

"Of course." She laughed.

He looked at her sideways. "I wanted to buy you a present. But C.J. wasn't as enthused about that."

"No kidding." Cari laughed again. She shook her head of wet curls. "You don't have to buy me any presents," she told him. "Just being here, taking care of Jamie, is enough."

He smiled as though he enjoyed her laughter. "The whole time, I wanted to be back here with you," he said softly.

She rolled her eyes. "Right." She turned away, bouncing Jamie in her arms.

"No, really. You don't believe that?"

Looking back at him, she flushed. She could see his honesty in his eyes. Yes, she believed it. But still, she didn't trust it. She sighed, remembering the morning kiss. If she didn't take care, they would be right back there again. She could see it in his eyes.

"Max, we have to talk."

"About not getting involved?" he asked gruffly.

She looked at him, marveling. What—did he read her mind?

"Exactly." She shook her head. "Especially if you're going to be marrying C.J. for heaven's sake."

"Marrying C.J." Slumping down onto the couch, he groaned, his head in his hands. "It's not going to be as easy as it seemed from a distance."

"You don't seem to like her very much."

"You can tell, can you?" He looked up, adorably cha-grinned, with his beautiful black hair falling over his eyes. "It's not really fair to say I don't like her. She's okay. For someone." He chuckled suddenly. "Randy, for instance."

She agreed, smiling. "He does seem to have a major crush there."

"Oh, yeah. He can't take his eyes off her."

She threw a hand up in the air. "Then let *him* marry her."

"Good idea. One flaw. That doesn't get me the ranch."

She dropped down beside him on the couch, sitting with her feet up on the coffee table and Jamie propped by her legs. The baby laughed at them both and they played with him for a moment. Then she turned to Max.

"Are you seriously considering marrying her just for her ranch?" It did seem a bit of a stretch.

"Yes, I am."

That was like a knife through her heart, though she knew it shouldn't matter to her at all.

"Why?"

He looked at her, his eyes clear and determined. "For my mother's sake."

He'd said something along these lines before but she had a hard time buying it. "Your mother tells you whom to marry?"

"No." He shook his head. "You don't understand."

She shrugged. "You got that right."

"Okay. I will try to explain."

"Please do."

He sat very still for a moment. She waited, her heart beating just a bit faster, anticipating what he might tell her. She knew it would involve heartbreak. When reasons seemed irrational, heartbreak was usually lurking somewhere in the mix.

"My brother, Gino, the one who died recently, he was just the best."

Max moved restlessly and Cari could see that this wasn't going to be easy for him to get through. He leaned forward, his elbows on his knees and his head in his hands. She resisted the impulse to reach out and run her fingers through his thick, lustrous hair.

"Gino did everything right. He was a skiing champion and a world-class swimmer. He danced like Fred Astaire and sang like Caruso. He was smart and good at business. He turned a small pair of cafés he took over when my uncle died into a major chain with restaurants all over Europe. He was handsome and loving, the sort of man whose smile was always his first reaction." His voice cracked, but he went on. "He was flawless."

Her breath caught in her throat. She gazed at Max with a compassion that threatened to overwhelm her.

"It's so tragic that you lost him."

"Yes." Clearing his throat, he looked up at her, his eyes dark and troubled. "But for my mother, it was more than tragedy. It was the end of her life."

Cari shook her head, confused. "But she still has you."

He nodded, but there was something that looked like anguish in his face. "Yes. Of course. But you see, it was Gino that she…" His voice trailed off and he looked away. For a moment he couldn't say the words. "Gino was the oldest, and he and my mother had a special bond. Gino was her helper when she went through some very bad things. I was too young to understand at the time, too young to be of much help. Gino was her right arm. When my father left her, she always said she couldn't have survived without Gino."

Cari frowned. She didn't really understand this. He was implying that his mother loved his brother more than anyone or anything—even Max himself. And yet she couldn't detect a bit of bitterness in him. He seemed to accept it in a way she'd never seen before. She didn't get it.

"Are you telling me you didn't resent her attitude?"

He looked up, shocked. "Resent it? Not at all. I felt the same way about him that she did. He was my best friend. He was my idol, my mentor, my guiding star. I would have given my life to save his."

Cari was struck by a sense of admiration. She wasn't used to a man who could put others before himself quite this way.

Brian had lived on bitterness. He always thought everyone he dealt with was out to cheat him and he tried to cheat them first, just to protect himself from their schemes. It had been hard to try to get him to see that others weren't really against him, because every attempt she made to do that just cast her in the role of his enemy, and he would accuse her of doing it, too.

Poor Brian. Now, at this distance, she could pity him. At the time, understanding had been harder to come by.

"My brother died trying out an experimental small plane. He was considering investing in the company that made it. It was a tremendous blow to us all, but to my mother, it was the end of her world. I had to have her closest servants watch her night and day to make sure she didn't take her own life. My heart was already broken by the death of my brother, but every time I saw the tragedy in her face, my heart would break again. I resolved that I would do anything—anything I could think of, to bring back her smile."

"And you think getting the ranch will do that?"

"Yes." He straightened and looked her full in the face. "I know it will. You see, her family settled the area where the Triple M Ranch is located in the nineteenth century. Her great-grandfather cleared the land. Her grandfather started the first profitable herd. She grew up on that ranch." He shook his head and his voice turned a little bitter. "And it was her own father who gambled away the family fortune and sold the ranch to C.J.'s father to keep from going to prison."

"I see."

"From the time I was a little boy, I was raised on stories of the Triple M. It just tortured my mother to think it was in C.J.'s family's hands instead of where it belonged. C.J.'s mother, Betty Jean, was my mother's best friend, but when C.J.'s father took over the ranch and then married Betty Jean, they broke all ties. My mother went to Europe and met and married my father. But she never got over losing the ranch."

"I think I'm beginning to understand some of the intensity here," Cari said tentatively, watching Jamie fall asleep propped against her legs. "But it still seems a bit extreme. Maybe it's an Italian thing?"

"My mother is as much a Texan as she is anything," he said with a crooked grin. "Maybe it's really a Texas thing."

She nodded, giving him that one. "Could be. We can be intense in our love for the land," she admitted.

"Anyway, a few weeks ago, C.J. wrote to my mother. She wanted to come to Italy for a visit." He frowned, thinking that over. "Okay, now I get it. Gino coming here last year, hoping he could buy the ranch, must have been what led her to believe we might be willing to do almost anything to get it back in our hands. So she decided to use it to leverage herself a husband."

"A rich husband," Cari reminded him.

"Of course. What good would a poor husband do for someone like C.J.?"

Cari shook her head. "You have a point there."

"Anyway, I didn't want her in Italy bothering my mother. And that was soon after Sheila called to tell me she'd had Gino's baby."

"And what did *she* want?"

"Just money. But when I demanded proof the baby was Gino's, she disappeared. It was a few weeks before my people traced her to Dallas. And that gave me a reason to come here to take care of two things at once."

That explained a lot of things, but it didn't make anything seem easier. Max needed to get the baby situation settled, and he needed to get control of the ranch. Both were up in the air right now. That was one thing she had to keep in mind. No matter how much she cared for him, no matter what happened between them, Max Angeli was just passing through. In another few days, he'd be gone. And maybe her life—and her heart— could get back to normal.

"So now I know why you parachuted by mistake into my life," Cari said with a tiny smile.

"Fate," he said. "Fate can be a—"

"Don't say it in front of the baby," she warned, rising and getting Jamie and his things together for the walk back to the nursery.

"Cari, Cari," he drawled, leaning back and looking at her languorously. "How long has it been since a man has made hot, sexy love to you?"

She threw him a sideways glance. "It's been so long that I'm not sure I remember what those words even mean."

"We should rectify that situation." There was a smile in his voice, but a thread of interest, as well, and a hint of sensual urgency that made her pulse race.

She gave him a quick smile and turned to leave. "No, thank you," she said back over her shoulder.

Laughing softly, he rose and followed her. "I forgot to tell you. C.J. and Randy are coming here for dinner."

"Oh? Down in the dining room?"

She assumed they would want to be away from the baby so they could have a relaxing evening. No matter. She would just as soon be up here, taking care of Jamie. She really didn't need any company.

"No," he said, surprising her. "Actually, C.J. wants to show Randy that she can cook. So she's going to prepare something wonderful on the little stove in the kitchenette."

Cari turned and stared at him. "What?"

"So she says." He grinned. "But we do have room service as a last resort."

She shook her head ruefully. "Somehow I'm afraid we're probably going to need it."

CHAPTER EIGHT

BUT Cari was wrong. C.J. turned out to be a wonderful cook, to the surprise of at least two of the dinner participants. She threw together plates of finger food, which included bite-size pieces of filet mignon on toast, salmon and crème fraîche on rye crackers, a light-as-air pâté on sautéed slices of croissant, lobster tail on sourdough bread rounds, bruschetta on deep-fried parmesan toast, and a few other things, each more delicious than the last.

"Appetizers," Max said without enthusiasm when she first put out her spread. But once he'd started eating, the only sounds to be heard were sighs of ecstasy.

"You see," C.J. said to Randy, flouncing her apron as she sashayed past. "I can cook. And on little tiny good-for-nothing stoves, too."

It turned out her purpose was to convince him that she could help him cater one of his large parties. He didn't need much more persuading once he'd tasted her food.

"Hire her," Max proclaimed, his mouth full of lobster. "She's a genius at cooking. This is wonderful stuff."

"I'm not trying to get a job with him," C.J. said pertly. "I'm trying to hire on with *you*, and you know it."

Max looked at the two women, one after the other, and inwardly he groaned. C.J. was gorgeous in an exaggerated way, all red lips and aggressive breasts and swinging hips, with fire-engine-red hair as icing on the very tempting cake. She was vivacious, exciting.

But—what the hell? He'd been there, done that. She was just like every other woman he'd dated since he was seventeen. He was bored with it, bored with her.

Cari was something new to him—warm, sweet, principled. She had standards. Imagine that! Rules she used to guide her life. He'd thought such things went out with high-buttoned shoes, except for boring, shriveled people who wanted to stop anyone from having fun.

But what Cari had was something different from anything he'd ever known. She had integrity. Wow. What a difference it made. Loving her would make him a better person. He knew that intuitively. She would change his life. Too bad it was so impossible.

Still she had a special spark that attracted him in a way C.J. and her type never could. What was he going to do about that? Or did he really need to do anything at all?

"That was the best meal I've had in ages, C.J.," Cari told her when the men had gone down to the bar for an after-dinner drink and left the women behind.

"My one talent," C.J. said with a sigh. "You see why I need to marry Max."

They were lounging on the couch, and Cari was feeling almost friendly to the woman.

"Do you really need to marry him?" she asked hesitantly. "I mean, after all, I'm sure he's willing to pay you quite a bit for the ranch. Why not just sell it to him and invest the money you get out of the deal?"

C.J. shook her head fervently. "No can do."

"Why not? You could get a lot of money for it."

"'Money' per se, isn't what I want. Security is what I need. The kind that major wealth can bring. That's my goal." She settled into the corner of the couch, pulling her legs up under her. "Here's a lesson in life, Cari. Money is very nice, but just plain old money has a way of slipping through your fingers. I've learned that often over the years. Money evaporates." She nodded wisely. "The land is always there. It's the goose that lays the golden egg. You don't sell off that darn old goose. Not if you're smart."

"So the ranch is doing well?" Cari asked, wondering just who was managing it. C.J. didn't seem to be doing it and she never seemed to talk about it.

"As well as can be expected. But that's not where I count on to get my support. It doesn't matter how much money the ranch makes. As I said, money can disappear in an instant. All kinds of things can make money disappear. Life can soak it right up. I've seen that happen. The ranch is my leverage. It's something I can use to get the life I want. I'm just lucky I've got it."

"I see."

"You know what?" C.J. went on. "This may surprise

you, but I'm tired of being a party girl. It's getting hard to keep up that front. Once my looks go, it'll be over anyway. I've got to prepare for my future. I want kids and a family just like everybody else."

"You do?" Cari stared at her. "I thought babies gave you the willies."

"They do. You don't think I'd be caught dead taking care of my children, do you? That's what servants are for."

"Oh. Why didn't I think of that?"

"Because you don't think ahead the way I do. You really should start planning for your own future, honey. I'm a bit older than you. I've been around the block a few times. I can teach you a few things." She nodded wisely and Cari tried to smile, but was afraid she wasn't very convincing.

"But as for me," she went on, "here's the bottom line. I want it all, but I don't want to do it grubbing in poverty. Max is my only hope for the good life. And I mean to take advantage of that hope any way I can."

Cari had to admire her honesty, even if she didn't think much of her ethics. Later, when C.J. and Randy had left, she told Max about what the woman had said.

"How well does that ranch do?" she asked him.

He shrugged. "The ranch is mortgaged to the hilt, from what I've been able to ascertain. They tell me she can't come up with the monthly fees at this point."

"Isn't there some way you can just sort of squeeze her out?"

He grinned at her terminology. "It's complicated. If this was an ordinary project, I wouldn't hesitate. That's how you make the big deals. But in this case, my mother wouldn't stand for it. She wants everything aboveboard and by the rules. She has a certain compassion for C.J."

Cari could understand that. For Max's mother, C.J. was a part of the Texas she'd left behind and still seemed to yearn for.

"So you'll have to marry her?"

He merely shrugged and looked deep into her eyes without saying anything. Finally he just walked away.

A half hour later, he asked if she'd like to come out to the ranch with him the next day.

"I want to go out to see it. Every time I ask C.J. to take me out, she finds a way to avoid it. I want to go out on my own and find out what she's trying to hide."

"Sure. We'll go with you." She didn't go anywhere without Jamie anymore.

"Good. I've ordered a picnic basket from the kitchen. We'd better leave early, just in case C.J. and Randy get a yen to visit again."

She laughed. She thought it was funny that Randy seemed to have attached himself to C.J. so thoroughly at the same time the woman thought she was romancing Max—sort of.

She left Max to watch a little television, and she went to bed, glad she had her own nightgown instead of the T-shirt. She was exhausted. Taking care of a baby was tiring work, even when you loved every minute of it. She quickly went to sleep and slept like a log until the wee hours.

Something woke her. She opened her eyes and for just a few seconds, wasn't sure where she was. Turning toward the crib, she saw a shadowy figure standing there and she gasped.

"Relax." It was Max. "It's only me. Jamie was whimpering, so I came in to make sure he was okay."

She reached out and turned on the bedside light and there he was, holding Jamie in his arms, the picture of the perfect dad. Joy filled her heart and tears sprang to her eyes.

"Oh, Max," she said, blubbering a bit.

"What's the matter?" He was astonished. "Did I frighten you that much? Cari, I'm sorry."

"No, it's not that." Slipping out of bed, she pulled her robe on and went to him, kissing his cheek and then smiling at the baby. "I'm just so happy," she said, choking on her words and smiling at him tearfully. "I just… it's just that my husband…" She sniffed and shook her head. "Never mind."

Max looked concerned. He started to put Jamie down in the crib but the baby was having none of it and started to whimper for real.

"Uh-oh," she said, looking down at the baby lovingly. "It looks like it's going to be one of those nights."

"One of what nights?" Max said as he pulled him back up into his arms.

"We're going to have to walk him."

"What do you mean?"

She smiled at him. "You'll see. I'll take the first shift. You can watch and learn." She shrugged. "Or go ahead and go back to bed," she added, giving him an out. "Whatever."

She changed his diapers and put on a fresh shirt and they tried putting him down to sleep again, but, just as she'd feared, he was totally awake and ready to play.

"No hope," she said cheerfully. "He going to need some coaxing to get back to sleep."

She pulled Jamie's blanket around him and put him to her shoulder, then started out toward the living room. Max followed close behind, slumping onto the couch as she began to pace with the baby in her arms.

"They love this," she told him. "The longer you walk, the happier they get."

"But do they go to sleep?"

"Ah, that's the question. That's why we're doing this. But sleep can be long in coming." She held Jamie close and kissed the top of his head. "There were nights I spent hours walking Michelle. Luckily, I think Jamie is a better sleeper than she was. He ought to go out pretty quickly."

He watched for a few minutes, then said quietly, "You've never told me much about your marriage, Cari. What was your husband like?"

"Brian?" She bit her lip. This wasn't one of her favorite topics. "He was just a guy."

"There's something I've wondered about," he went on. Rising, he met her on one of her passes and took her hand in his, spreading her fingers. "No rings. Why is that? As a widow, I would think you would want to have that sort of memento of your marriage."

She stared at her own hand and nodded slowly.

"I used to have rings."

"What happened to them?"

She looked up into his face. "I sold them."

He narrowed his eyes, searching her face as though he wanted to understand. "You sold your rings?"

"Yes."

Jamie began to stir, and she pulled her hand away from Max so that she could start pacing again.

"I had a beautiful wedding set with a very pretty diamond," she went on as she walked. "But I sold them. They went to pay for me finishing college and starting on my real estate license." She smiled at the irony of it all. "Brian never knew that he financed my new start in life."

Max had a point about the rings. If she'd valued her marriage, she would have kept them, no matter how tight money got. But she couldn't really grieve for Brian, not the way she knew she should. By the time he'd died, she'd known she was going to have to leave him one way or another.

He'd made life with him impossible and had pretty much killed the love she'd once had for him. When she thought about it now she couldn't believe she'd stayed as long as she had. What had kept her with him once she'd known he was getting more and more irrational? The fear of admitting failure, she supposed.

"So you're getting a real estate license?" he noted, interested that she would have chosen a field so close to his. "Why? Residential real estate is dead as the proverbial doornail in most areas right now."

"I know. But real estate always comes back. And I want to be ready when that happens."

He nodded, glad for the evidence that she was an optimist. He liked that about her.

She smiled at him. "In the meantime, I don't mind working as a waitress. It's honest work and I can make a decent living as long as I only have myself to take care of."

Jamie chose that moment to begin happily making motorboat noises. They both laughed.

"It doesn't sound like he's falling asleep," Max said.

"Not yet," she replied. "It takes a while sometimes."

"Let me take my turn," he said, reaching for the baby. "You sit down and tell me about your marriage," he said.

She gazed into his eyes. "Why do you want to know?" she wondered.

He touched her cheek with the palm of his hand. "Because I care about you," he said simply. And as he said the words, he knew it was true. He'd never known a woman like Cari before, never had a relationship like this. He liked her. He wanted to talk to her. He wanted to know more about her. That had never happened with a woman before. But it felt right.

"Sit. And talk." He began to pace with Jamie cuddled nicely in his arms.

She sat. She usually hated to talk about the past. But tonight the words just started to flow out.

"I knew Brian for years. All through high school. I had no excuse." She sighed. Wasn't that the truth? It was amazing how one could delude oneself. "I knew what he was like. But I had the young girl's syndrome, thinking love would conquer all, marriage would change him, I would change him, my love would show him the way."

"Change him how?" Max asked.

"Change him from being a jerk, I suppose," she said with a short laugh. "Change him into a decent person and a good husband and father. It didn't happen, of course."

"It hardly ever does," he agreed.

She nodded. "Living with Brian was like living with a human geyser. You never knew what might set him off, but you knew he was going to blow. And it was over something different every time."

Max's tone was tense. "Was he violent with you?"

She hesitated. What was the point of going over all that? "Only a little."

She could see the veins in Max's neck cord and she hurried to add, "I knew where it all stemmed from. His father was an alcoholic and he had a very rough childhood. You always think that love and goodness will heal things like that. And they so seldom do. It's just not enough to overcome the damage that sort of childhood does."

It was funny. She'd never told anyone, even Mara, all these details. So why was she telling Max? Of all the people in the world, he was probably the one who least needed to know these things about her. But it was such a relief to tell someone about it.

"I don't want to make it sound like unrelieved agony. It wasn't like that at all. There were many good times. He could make me laugh. And he loved the baby." Her voice softened as she thought of her baby. "Michelle was a perfect baby, all pink and plump and smiling. He was so proud of her. And yet…" Her voice got a little rough.

"When she cried, he would go crazy. He couldn't stand it. It almost seemed as though he thought she was trying to get to him on purpose. He took it personally. I would do everything I could to keep her from crying." She choked as painful memories surged. "Sometimes he would smash things," she said, her voice barely above a whisper. "And then he would leave."

Max stopped in front of her, staring down. "But he didn't hurt you? Or the baby?"

"Not…not really." She was skimming over the truth a bit here, but she really didn't want to dredge all that up again. "I was afraid of that, though. He would just get so irrational. There was no telling what he would do eventually. That last night, he was so angry."

She closed her eyes as she remembered, and her voice became almost robotic.

"He grabbed Michelle and raced out to the car with her. I ran after him, pleading with him to leave her, but he threw her into the backseat and started the car up. She was screaming at the top of her lungs. I was frantic. I managed to get into the car before he had time to lock the doors. We took off down the street. I was trying to climb over the seat to get into the back to take care of Michelle when he…he…" She closed her eyes again, seeing it as though it were yesterday. "We crashed into a fence and then a tree."

She took a shuddering breath and looked up into his face. His beautiful eyes were filled with compassion and reflected her pain. Somehow that was so comforting.

"It could have been my fault," she hurried to add. "I'm just not sure. The way I was climbing over the seat, only thinking about getting to Michelle, not about how I might be interfering with his driving. I can't put all the blame on Brian."

Max snorted. "I can," he muttered, beginning to walk again.

"I was in the hospital for about a week. A couple of broken ribs and injuries to a few internal organs." She shrugged. "I got better. They didn't." She took a deep breath. "They didn't tell me that Brian and Michelle were dead at first. I kept asking for her."

Tears filled her eyes and she shook her head angrily. She didn't want to cry. She'd done enough crying to fill an ocean, and she'd thought she didn't have any more tears to give. But there were always more.

Max was leaving the room. She blinked after him.

"Where are you going?"

"He's asleep," he told her softly. "I'm putting him in his crib."

She nodded, rising to follow him. By the time she got to the nursery, he'd put Jamie down and covered him. He turned and took her in his arms, raining kisses on her face and muttering something in Italian.

She laughed with tears still filling her eyes. When he kissed her, she kissed him back, giving him her passion as well as her joy. But only for a moment.

"No," she said, pulling away from him. "Max, no."

He said something in Italian. She didn't understand the words, but she knew his meaning. She shook her head.

"No," she said again. "Max, you're going to marry C.J. You're going to belong to another woman. We can't."

This time the Italian was a curse word she fully understood, but he released her, only to grab her hand and hold it up.

"You should have rings," he said with Italian intensity. "You should have beautiful jewelry to match your beautiful eyes. You should be draped in diamonds."

She laughed aloud. What a concept!

"I don't need jewelry," she told him. "It just gets in the way."

He shook his head in disgust at her attitude, and then he kissed her again. Gently but firmly, she pushed him away and led him to the door of the room.

"Good night, Max," she told him, her growing affection for the man shining in her eyes. "Better get some sleep."

"Yes," he reluctantly agreed. "Don't forget. We're driving out to the ranch in the morning."

"I'll be up early," she promised.

He gave her a crooked grin. "So will I. We have no choice. We play by Jamie's rules these days, don't we?"

The drive to the ranch went through some beautiful Texas landscape. Max filled the time with stories his mother had told him over the years of adventures she'd had growing up in the Texas countryside, stories that made it sound like an ideal place for an old-fashioned upbringing. But the arrival, when it came, was anticlimactic.

"This can't be it," Max said, staring at the dilapidated buildings on a hill that appeared to stand at the end of the driveway leading up from the highway where the Triple M Ranch sign hung by one corner on a rusty archway.

There was a gate, but it gave easily to a little push from the nose of the car. They drove slowly up the long entry. Straggly trees lined the way, only a few of them still alive. The buildings were empty. It was pretty obvious no one had been living there for quite some time.

"I don't see any sign of cattle," Max said, shielding his eyes from the sun as he gazed out over the dusty plains surrounding the hill. "This doesn't even look like a working ranch." He shook his head. "And this certainly doesn't look like the ranch my mother told me about all my life. They've let it go to hell. It's a damn shame."

Cari could see how disappointed he was. "Maybe we came to the wrong side of the property," she suggested.

He shook his head. "No. This seems to be it. No wonder C.J. didn't want me coming out here."

"Well, we can have our picnic here at least," she said, beginning to unload the car and set up a shaded place for Jamie.

Max agreed, though he was grouchy about it. She felt sorry for him, but she couldn't help but wonder how this was going to impact his plans. If this made him look at things more realistically, maybe it was all for the best.

They spread out a ground cloth under a tree and opened up the picnic basket to find fried chicken and biscuits and corn on the cob.

"In February?" Max said, looking at the corn suspiciously.

"It's either imported or frozen," Cari agreed. "Not quite up to the quality you expect in the good old summertime, but it tastes pretty good."

They ate and chatted and played with Jamie, and gradually Max's mood improved. He got to the point where he could see some of the good things in the land around him, such as the wildflowers just beginning to poke up their heads, and the white, puffy clouds scudding by in a pure blue sky.

"You know, I have to admit, this place could have fit in with my mother's stories in better times. But beyond that, I had a different picture of the ranch in mind."

"Did you?"

"Yes. I realize now it wasn't even based on what she'd told me. I watched that TV show. What was the name of that ranch on it? Southfork? Well, that was sort of the picture I had in my mind. A big house. A big barn. Lots of big cars parked out front. A helicopter pad out back. Miles and miles of expensive fencing. Some cattle, maybe."

She smiled, nodding. "I've seen the show."

"Even though this might have been an impressive place in its day," he said, "it was never like Southfork. Still, it was probably a good working ranch. Too bad that time seems to be long past." He grimaced. "I'm glad my mother isn't here to see this. I hope no one ever tells her about it."

They drove back to the city, taking the long way and enjoying the scenery. Max's mobile chimed and he pulled over to take the call. He looked serious as he listened, but Cari was playing with Jamie and didn't pay too much attention. When he'd hung up, he turned to her.

"Bad news," he said shortly. "Sheila won't be coming back." His gaze flickered over Jamie and he winced slightly. "They found her body in the river. Seems to be drug related."

"Oh, Max!"

They both looked at the child who was happily playing with a ring of plastic keys, totally oblivious to the fate of his mother. Then they looked at each other and without a word, came together for a long embrace. This was a tragedy for a baby, but at least he was too young to understand what an earthshaking event had just contorted his life. Perhaps it was best that way.

Back in town, Max made some calls and came up with more news.

"The police haven't been able to find any relatives for Sheila, and neither have any of my people." He looked deeply into Cari's eyes. "Everything is going to ride on the DNA results."

She laced her fingers under her chin as she considered that. "And if they come back negative?"

He looked pained. "Cari, if that happens, it will be out of my hands. If I have no marriage or blood ties to Jamie, there is nothing I can do. I'll have no right to keep him here." He shook his head. "Even all those lawyers I pay so much money to won't be able to fix that one."

She shrunk back. "So he would go into the county system."

"I imagine so."

If that happened...

Oh, it couldn't happen. Blindly, she turned and hurried back to the nursery. Jamie was sound asleep, but she had to hold him. Hadn't there been a time she'd vowed not to fall in love? That time seemed very long ago.

CHAPTER NINE

"As I UNDERSTAND it, tomorrow is Valentine's Day."

Cari straightened as Max came into the nursery two days later. She gave him a mischievous smile.

"You are correct, sir," she replied.

He stood gazing down at her, a twinkle in his eyes.

"Is it true that this is a fairly important day to women in this country?" he asked.

She frowned, wondering what the catch was going to be. "Well, it can be."

"Good." He smiled like the proverbial cat. "I've made arrangements."

"Arrangements?" Did she really have to hear about the details? "Are you going to do something with C.J.?"

His dark gaze was like velvet. "No. I'm going to do something with you."

"Me." Her eyes widened. Why not C.J.? Wasn't that the woman he was supposedly going to marry? Maybe not. She knew he'd been working on that for the past few days.

"There's got to be a way to convince her to sell that

wreck of a ranch," he'd fumed more than once. "I'm willing to pay her twice what it's worth. And I want her to close on this as soon as possible. I want to begin renovating the place before my mother finds out what a mess it's in."

"She claims she'll never sell."

He'd stared at her with haunted eyes. "She has to sell," he'd said. "She'll do it. If I can just find the right approach." But he didn't sound very convincing.

And now he was talking about taking her to a romantic dinner instead of C.J.

"I can't go anywhere," she protested. "I've got to be here for Jamie."

He nodded. "We're going to bring him along."

She gazed at him suspiciously. "Where are we going?"

He raised an eyebrow. "Nowhere."

"What?"

He grinned, chucking her under the chin. "It's a surprise. You wait and see."

And then he was gone.

She sighed, half laughing. Anyone watching the two of them over the past few days would swear they were lovers. And in truth, she felt like his lover. The only things missing were commitment and some honest-to-goodness lovemaking. But neither of those things could happen with C.J. lurking in the wings.

And of course there was the constant awareness that this was a passing fancy, something meant to last for days, not years or a lifetime. But she was intrigued that he meant to celebrate Valentine's Day with her and not with C.J. And just what would C.J. have to say about that, she wondered?

The phone call came the next afternoon, just as Cari began getting ready for their Valentine's dinner. The DNA test results were in. Max was asked to meet with a panel of lab technicians and legal representatives, and he left right away. Cari stayed behind and worried.

They'd had a small memorial service for Sheila. C.J. and Randy had come. Cari had taken Jamie as well, just so someone could tell him in later years that he had been to a ceremony honoring his mother's life, even if he had no idea what it was all about at the time.

And now they were going to find out whether Jamie would be staying with Max, where Cari was completely sure he belonged, or not. It was nail-biting time. She went into the nursery and watched Jamie sleeping. If they had to give this adorable child up, surely she wouldn't be able to stand it.

She heard Max come in and she ran to the front room. One look at his face told her all she needed to know. The test had come in with a positive match. With a shriek of joy, she ran to him and he swung her up in the air, both of them laughing with happiness. Tears streamed down her face. It was the best moment she'd had in many years.

They went into the nursery and Max looked down at the little child who carried his brother's legacy. Finally he was free to let his heart fill with love for the boy without reservation. This was truly a special day.

"The first thing I need to do is call my mother," he noted.

"Not now," she protested. "The time difference."

He shook his head. "She won't care. Not when she hears what I'm calling about."

"Does she have any idea that there is a baby?"

"No. I didn't want to get her hopes up so I never told her about Sheila's claim." He grinned, shaking his head. "This is just incredible, isn't it? I can hardly believe it."

Cari nodded happily. She was bound and determined not to let herself think about the fact that this meant it was the beginning of the end for her and her connection to Max. She would think about that tomorrow. Tonight, they would just enjoy the news.

"Now we really have something to celebrate," Max said.

Two hours later he was leading her, with Jamie in the stroller, to the elevator.

"Did you talk to your mother?" she asked.

"No. It turns out she is staying with a friend. But I left a message for her to call me as soon as she gets my message."

"Good. Now tell me. Where are we going?"

He shook his head, eyeing her with thinly veiled affection. "My lips are sealed. I ought to put a blindfold on you. That way you might actually be surprised."

"No blindfolds," she said. "I promise to be as surprised as I need to be."

She'd assumed they would be eating somewhere in the hotel, but she hadn't realized it would be a private conference room. When he opened the double doors to let them enter, she gasped. Max had ordered up decorations, and the staff had filled the room with red and white balloons, with white lacy streamers hanging from the rafters and beautiful potted trees covered with white and red birds in each corner. A small table was set with delicate china and gleaming silver. In the corner, a guitarist was setting up his music and soon was playing soft, romantic melodies.

Cari was enchanted. She'd never seen anything more beautiful. She turned to Max, her eyes shining.

"Happy Valentine's Day," he said.

"Oh, Max, thank you. This is lovely."

He dropped a kiss on her lips and then escorted her to her place at the table and rolled the stroller up next to her. Luckily, Jamie had fallen asleep as soon as they had started on their journey through the hotel, so she would have some time to devote to Max and the wonderful dinner he'd ordered up. She tucked the blanket around the baby, then straightened and noticed a long, flat velvet box had been set in front of her.

"Max," she said warningly.

"Just a little Valentine's present," he said.

Her heart was beating in her throat as she pulled open the box, then drew her breath in sharply. She was almost blinded by the flash of fire from diamonds—more diamonds than she'd ever seen in one place before.

"What…?"

"Let me help you."

He came behind her to put on the necklace. It was surprisingly light for something with so many diamonds. She looked at her own reflection in the mirror on the other side of the room and she could hardly breathe. She'd never seen anything so beautiful.

"And to go with the necklace…" He reached into the pocket of his suit coat and pulled out a matching bracelet. "One without the other would be incomplete," he said as he put it on her wrist.

"Oh, Max." She was stunned and overwhelmed. "Oh, Max, I can't—"

"Yes, you can," he said firmly. Going down on one knee so that he could look into her eyes, he was adamant. "Cari, don't insult me by refusing my gift. I can well afford it. You don't have to feel any special obligation or gratitude or anything like that. It's just a gift. A token of my affection for you. And you know very well that's for real."

He kissed her gently, softly, and with a purity of emotion she could hardly stand to accept. It was like looking into the sun. It was almost too much to bear.

Looking at his face, she realized how much more than handsome he was. There was honesty and integrity there, and an earnest desire to make her happy. Her heart was full. Yet she was uncertain.

"But I don't need gifts to prove that," she protested.

"No, you don't need them. But it makes me happy to give you diamonds. Can you allow me that happiness?"

She looked at him in wonder, and then she laughed. "Oh, Max," she said. "Do you always get your way?"

"Of course."

Dinner was served, and it consisted of a wonderful Italian pork dish in a pinot noir reduction sauce along with a cheesy pasta to die for. There was also a lovely salad and the pièce de résistance—a heart-shaped baked Alaska. They ate with gusto and sipped red wine and talked and laughed, and when the meal was over, they danced to the music the guitarist played.

Diamonds glittered when she moved and the reflections of their light flashed against the walls of the room. It almost seemed a counterpart to the way Max's touch sizzled on her skin. It had been a magical evening, but she knew it was drawing to a close. If only there was some way to keep it going all night.

"This is the most perfect Valentine's Day I've ever had," she told him simply.

"Good." He dropped a kiss on her lips. "Not too ordinary?" he teased.

She shook her head. "Not a bit ordinary," she said. Reaching up, she touched his face with the flat of her hand. "Oh, Max," she began, feeling the need to express to him how she felt.

But she never got the chance. Before she could get another word out, C.J.'s voice was booming through the room.

"So this is what you're up to, is it? I should have known."

There she stood, hands on her hips, green eyes flashing angry fire.

"C.J." Max started toward her. "What are you doing here?"

"Looking for you. What else? It's Valentine's Day. But I see you know that." She glared at him. "Don't you think you should have been with me? I'm the one you're supposed to marry."

Max stopped dead and stared at her coldly. "C.J., I haven't made any sort of commitment to you and you know it."

"It's her, isn't it?" she cried, pointing at Cari. "It's because of her. You've fallen in love with her, haven't you?" Swinging around, she faced Cari. "If it wasn't for you, we could have this whole deal done by now." She took a step toward Cari, shaking her head as though she were beseeching her. "Look, I've stood back and I've been tolerant. I knew he went for you, not me. That was okay. I figured, if he wants to have some fun on the side, let him. That doesn't bother me at all. But I want the wedding ring on my finger, I want the marriage certificate in my hand. Then he can do whatever he wants."

"C.J., you're embarrassing yourself," Max told her quietly, controlling his temper with obvious effort.

"Oh, yeah?" She tossed her flaming hair back and glared. "Well, get this, mister. This is it. No more Ms.

Nice Guy. I want a wedding date and I want it now. Or you can forget about your mother getting back her beloved ranch."

Max looked pained. "Go home, C.J. You weren't invited here."

Her face reddened in outrage. "Be careful, Max. My patience is not infinite."

"Good. It shouldn't be. And in that vein, let me explain more explicitly." He stood before her, legs apart, arms at his sides. "I'm not going to marry you. Not ever. And if that means my mother will have to forgo having her ranch back, that is the price we will have to pay."

C.J.'s head went back, but her glare didn't dim.

He shook his head, exasperated with her. "But you know very well we aren't in love with each other. And even more important, we don't suit each other at all. We would both be miserable tied together by a wedding vow. Upon reflection, I've decided it would be a very bad move. So it's out. Sorry."

On a certain level, Cari felt sorry for the woman. She'd made her intentions clear from the beginning. It was too bad she hadn't noticed earlier that her plans were just not panning out. Cari was watching the scene carefully and she saw the anger in C.J.'s face. Anger and frustration. But no pain, no sadness. This failure had touched her spirit, but not her heart. That relieved Cari somewhat.

Randy appeared out of nowhere and was helping to get C.J. out of the room, though she was still railing at Max.

Valentine's Day was over. And just in time, Jamie woke up.

CHAPTER TEN

IT WAS a good hour later before they settled down and got Jamie back to sleep, in his bed this time. Cari was still trying to come to terms with what had happened. Max had pretty much rejected the plan to marry C.J. Did he mean it? And what did that mean for the prospects of getting his mother the ranch? She couldn't help but worry.

Max was taciturn and restless, sitting on the couch not watching the television which played in the background. She knew he was thinking over the ramifications of what he'd just done. She slid onto the couch beside him and took his hand in hers.

"Max, you always say that you came to Dallas with two big goals in mind. Number one was to find your brother's son and to find proof that he is Gino's. And you've done that. You've saved Jamie's life and you are going to have a beautiful baby who will carry on Gino's memory and be a part of your family forever. You're giving your mother a gift of love that can't be equaled.

Jamie will remind you and your family every day of what a wonderful brother you had."

Max inclined his head, acknowledging everything she'd said as his fingers curled around hers. "You had a part in it all," he mentioned, but she waved that away.

"Your second goal was to return the ownership of the family ranch to your mother because losing it had preyed on her mind for years and you thought it would make her happy to have control of it again, something to help heal the unhealable wound losing Gino had dealt her. This you haven't achieved as yet."

"True."

Now came the hard part. "You know you could achieve it by marrying C.J."

He nodded. "But that's not going to happen."

She frowned, shaking her head. "Then how are you going to get control of the ranch?"

He grimaced and shrugged. "I'll find another way."

That chilled her. What if desperation drove him to do something illegal, or even underhanded in some way? She knew that would eat away at him. She couldn't let something like that happen. But what could she do? When it came right down to it, this was none of her business. Why was she even delving into it?

Because she wanted to help him. Because she was worried about him. Because…and this was the bottom line…she was in love with him.

Yes, it was true, and she had to admit it to herself.

She'd fallen in love with the man she'd vowed to harden her heart to from the start. What a fool she was.

Turning, she looked at his handsome face, and some of her self-criticism faded. He was so gorgeous and so good and so lovable. How could she not fall for a man like this?

Especially now as he moved closer and he took her chin in his hand and he began to kiss her mouth with quick, hungry nips that made her gasp. Ordinarily she would pull away. Ordinarily she would protest. But he wasn't marrying C.J. anymore. So she was going to give in to temptation for just a few minutes. It just felt so good.

His hands held her head on either side now, and his kisses were growing deeper and more urgent. Reaching up, she dug her fingers into his thick hair and arched her breasts against him. He was so very male and she was so very female and they were caught up in a dance as old as life. Every part of her body began to relax, and then to tingle with pleasure. She wanted his hands on her breasts, and his lips, too. She wanted to feel him crush her to the couch with his hard body. She wanted all of him.

The phone rang. For a moment she thought he was going to ignore the sound of the phone and make love to her instead. That was what she wanted. That was what he wanted, too. But in the back of her mind she knew this had to be his mother. Gathering all her strength, she pushed back and startled him into noticing.

"It's going to be your mother," she panted, pulling her clothing together. "You'd better take it."

"I'll call her later," he muttered, kissing her again.

"No, Max. You'll hate yourself if you don't take this call."

It took another minute for him to come to his senses, but when he did, he rose and took the phone call. She sat on the couch and smiled as she listened to their conversation. It was in half in Italian, but she understood every word and every emotion. As Max explained about Jamie, the astonished joy on the other side of the Atlantic was easy to feel. It was a good night.

And a lucky phone call. If his mother hadn't interrupted, she might have made love with Max. Her willpower had eroded beyond usefulness for a moment there. She had it back now. She knew it would be crazy to make love with a man, no matter how much you loved him, without some sort of plan or commitment. And she had neither. So she was going to give him one last kiss and go off to her bed—alone. Sighing, she turned and prepared to do just that.

Cari was juggling baby bottles and Jamie the next morning when her phone rang. It was Mara.

"Did you have a nice Valentine's Day?" she asked hopefully.

Cari smiled into the phone. "It was wonderful."

"Good. I'm so glad we fixed that." Mara sighed happily. "So, where did you and Randy go last night?"

It had been a while since she'd talked to her friend. Her heart sank as she realized Mara didn't have a clue as to what had been going on. How was she going to tell her?

"Mara, I didn't go out with Randy."

There was a shocked pause, then Mara cried, "What? But I talked to him and he said…"

"If he said he was out for Valentine's, he must have been out with C.J."

"C.J.?" Her voice was rising. "Who is C.J.?"

Mara was sounding a bit tightly wound at this point. Cari tried to use a soothing tone.

"You remember about C.J. She's the other woman in the big mix-up."

"Oh. Ah. And so I imagine you were out with the other man?" She was back to being hopeful again.

"Yes. Max Angeli."

Mara laughed. "Okay, I can hear it in the way you say his name. You're in love, aren't you?"

She never gave up. Cari was halfway between laughter and outrage.

"No!"

Mara nagged at her for another twenty minutes but, Cari wouldn't break down and admit it, not even to her best friend—even though she was very much afraid it was true.

And if it was true, just what exactly was she going to do about it?

There wasn't really much she could do. Max had told C.J. he wouldn't marry her last night, but in the bright light of morning, she couldn't take that seriously.

She knew him well enough by now to know he would do anything he had to do to heal his mother's heart. And that was one of the things she loved about him.

She gave Jamie a bath and cleaned his room and put him in an adorable baby suit. But all the while, her mind was on the facts, and the facts were stubborn things.

She had to face them. She had to be realistic. Max had a lot of affection for her. He enjoyed being with her. And he definitely wanted her in his bed—he'd made that perfectly clear. But he'd never said one word about marrying her, had he? He hadn't even contemplated that as much as he had contemplated marrying C.J. Marriage of any sort did not seem to be on his horizon.

He'd made it clear from the beginning that he wasn't the marrying kind. And she'd told him much the same about herself. Too bad she'd changed her mind. He obviously hadn't.

And no, she couldn't see herself as a paid mistress, traveling to Venice with the family, being with Max as long as his interest lasted, then segueing into the role of nanny once he'd moved on to someone else.

Ugh. That picture didn't fit at all. There was no way she could live her life like that. Painful as it was, she was going to have to withdraw from the field. There was no other way.

But how could she leave Max? She knew now that she loved him. And how could she leave Jamie? She loved Jamie almost as much as she'd loved Michelle. Well, she'd survived losing her own baby. Now she would have to develop ways to live through losing Jamie—but with a broken heart that might never be repaired.

She tried to talk to Max about it the next day when he came home for lunch. He brought in burgers in a sack and they sat down at the dining-room table to eat out of cardboard containers. She mentioned a few things obliquely at first, venturing carefully into the subject, but he dismissed it out of hand.

"I'm not marrying C.J.," he stated firmly. "I'll find another way to get the ranch. And I want you here with Jamie. That's all there is to it."

She licked her lips and tried to think of a way to make him understand. "I think I should go. I have a feeling you would be better able to negotiate with C.J. if I was out of the picture."

He was astonished and not very happy to hear this theory. "I don't want you out of the picture. I need you in my life."

"Max, there's no room for me in your life. It's already too crowded in there. You've got too much going on as it is."

He dismissed that with a wave of his hand. "Cari, C.J. is irrational. She wants things that cannot be. Whether you are here or not, she is still going to want those things."

Cari shook her head, looking troubled. "I don't know. I think my being here puts her back up and makes her more rigid in her demands. If I were gone she might be more reasonable."

"Yes, but I wouldn't be," he noted dryly. "If you were gone, I'd be a bear to live with."

He was teasing and not really taking what she was saying seriously. She could understand that. He didn't want her to go, so he was rationalizing that it was for the best that she stay. But she felt she could see things a little more clearly. She had to go.

Max left for a meeting with the lawyers, and she called Mara and got the number of the person she used for babysitting. Calling her, she made arrangements for the woman to come right over and begin taking care of Jamie. Then she went into the nursery and pulled out the velvet box with the necklace and bracelet inside. She looked at it for a long moment, sliding her hand over the surface. Then she pressed it to her cheek and closed her eyes, remembering how it felt to dance with Max while a guitar played in the background. It had been a wonderful night she would never forget. But it was over. Bracing herself, she walked briskly into Max's room and left the velvet box on his dresser.

She spent an hour showing the babysitter where everything was and getting Jamie used to her. And then she packed all her belongings into one suitcase on wheels and took one last look around the hotel suite. She'd only lived there for a little over a week, but it had become home very quickly. She was going to miss it.

And the emotion she was going to feel when she left Jamie behind didn't bear thinking of. Her heart dropped every time she did think of it. But she had to do what she had to do. And finally, it was time.

She'd barely made it to the hallway when the elevator dinged. Tensing, she waited to see if Max was back. But it wasn't Max. An older woman got off the elevator and started her way.

Max's mother. It had to be.

Cari watched her for a moment. A tall, regal-looking woman, she seemed more European elite than Texas rancher. Where was the evidence of that wild young girl who had ridden bareback over the plains and hunted rattlesnakes with the boys?

"Hello," she said, her eyes friendly as she looked at Cari. "I'm looking for the suite that belongs to Max Angeli. Can you direct me?"

"Of course," she said. "Please come this way." She escorted her to the door and rang the bell. "Someone will let you in any moment," she said, and as the woman turned to face the door, she added, sotto voce, "I'm in love with your son."

"What is that, my dear?" she said, turning back to look at her curiously.

Cari shook her head and smiled. "Nothing," she said. "It was nice to meet you, Mrs. Angeli."

She walked away quickly, not waiting for a reply.

It was almost comforting to be back at work at the café—the same old routine, the same old people—she'd missed it all. It felt so nice and ordinary. There was that word again. That made her laugh, and then it made her tear up. Ordinary. That was exactly what she was.

All the diamonds and the luxury rooms and the fancy foods—that was for some other person, not for her. She belonged here in ordinaryland.

Mara was upset, of course. "Well, there's still Randy," she pointed out when Cari told her what had happened.

"Oh, Mara, please! He's head over heels in love with C.J. You should see him mooning after her."

"But if she goes off with Max—"

"No. That won't work. You see, the whole situation was never going to be Max and C.J. setting up housekeeping. She just wanted to be his wife for all the rights and privileges—and money—and wasn't expecting to fulfill any of the responsibilities. She made it perfectly plain that was never in the cards. I'll tell you, from what I've seen, I think she prefers Randy when you come right down to it. She can boss him around."

On the first day back at work, she kept looking at the entry doors, expecting to see Max come strolling through. But he didn't come. And he didn't come the next day, either. By the third day she had pretty much decided she must have dreamed the whole thing. Maybe there really wasn't such a person as Max Angeli. Maybe Jamie was a manifestation of her grief. Who knew?

She'd been so sure she would never love again. She'd been so sure that she was too wary to let another man steal her heart. But she'd thrown all that to the winds and fallen for Max. Now she was back to square one, but with a new crack down the center of her heart. Hopefully, she'd learned something. Why did lessons like this have to hurt so much?

On the fourth day she was talking a cowboy into having a piece of lemon meringue pie when a lovely older woman entered the café. Cari didn't recognize her at first, as she wouldn't have expected to see her there in the café in a hundred years. But she knew right away she'd seen her before, and for just a second, she assumed it was a movie star or a TV performer. Then she realized it was Max's mother.

Max's mother. Her first thought was something had happened, something bad. But that fear died quickly. The woman looked too calm, too sanguine.

She came up and took a seat at the counter.

"Hello," she said as her gaze met Cari's.

"Mrs. Angeli," Cari said a bit breathlessly, wiping her hands on her apron and hoping her hair wasn't too wild.

"You recognize me." She smiled.

"Of course. I'm…"

"Cari Christensen. Yes, I know." She reached out and shook Cari's hand. "I just felt I should come in and say hello to you and thank you for all you did to help settle my grandson into his new life."

"It was my pleasure. How is he?"

"Wonderful. Perfect. We couldn't be happier."

"I'm so glad." They smiled at each other.

"I'm sure he'd like to see you again."

Cari's smile faded. "I'd love to see him, too. But I don't think it would be a good idea."

"I understand. Breaking away is so hard."

"Yes."

She ordered a piece of chocolate cake and a glass of milk. Cari wondered if that was what she used to order as a girl whenever she came into town. But the café was filling up, and Cari was too busy to talk any longer. When she looked up a bit later, Mrs. Angeli was gone.

It was the next day that Max came in.

"Hi," he said, his gaze never leaving her face from the moment he entered the café.

"Hi."

He stood before her, his eyes luminous. "I've missed you."

She could hardly breathe. "Me, too."

Reaching out, he cupped her cheek with his hand.

"Max, don't," she whispered helplessly.

He shrugged and drew his hand back.

"Can I get you anything?" she asked.

"Sure," he said, sliding onto a seat at the counter. "How about a piece of apple pie?"

"Coming right up."

It was good to have something to do with her hands. They were shaking. She put a piece of pie on a plate and carried it over to where he was sitting.

"Thanks."

"You're welcome."

She stood watching him as he ate, her heart beating in her throat. Why was he here? And why hadn't he come looking for her sooner? But she knew the answer to that. He had other things on his mind. Like the ranch. Like C.J.

"I hear my mother came in to see you," he said suddenly, looking up.

"Yes, she did."

He had a slight smile. "She liked you."

Cari's smile was bigger. "That's nice. I liked her, too." She hesitated, then added, "She said Jamie was doing well."

"Oh, yeah. She adores him."

"Of course."

They smiled at each other, agreement about Jamie's wonderfulness warming the connection between them.

"He's going to be the most spoiled baby in Dallas."

"I'm sure of it."

"And the ranch? Has she been out there?"

He pushed the pie plate away. "See, here's the funny thing. I didn't want her to go. I was scared to death to have her see what a dump it was. But she insisted, so we packed up and went out there. C.J. even came along."

"And? Was she devastated?"

He shook his head. "Not at all. In fact, as far as she's concerned, it looks a lot like it looked when she lived there."

Cari's jaw dropped. "No!"

He grinned. "She was ecstatic. She went running around exploring every nook and cranny, remembering when she'd hidden under the front porch when trying to get out of chores or where she'd found an arrowhead near the well. She told C.J. stories about her mother she'd never known before, showed her where she and Betty Jean had snuck out to go to a dance in town when they weren't supposed to, things like that."

Cari was astounded. The place was such a dump. "How did C.J. like that?"

"She was very touched. She was crying half the time."

"C.J.?"

He nodded. "In fact, she's selling us the ranch."

A wave of emotion hit her hard and she was light-headed. "No kidding," she said breathlessly. This was huge. But what did it mean?

"She and Randy are going to use the money to fund an expansion of his catering business. They want to be the biggest caterer in Texas." He shrugged, looking up at her. "I think they'll get married."

Cari had to grip the edge of the counter to keep from falling over. "Wow. Well, more power to them." She blinked rapidly, wondering why he was torturing her this way. "And you? Are you going back to Venice soon?"

"Yes." His gaze was black as coal. "We're getting ready to go this weekend. Just for a few days, though. We'll be back."

"Oh," she said faintly.

He rose from his seat. "Well, I'd better get going. I've got a lot of packing to do. Jamie's got enough stuff to fill a plane on his own by now."

"I imagine." Her heart sank. He was going. So that was it, then. It really was over.

"Cari?"

"Hmm?" She looked up, feeling bereft.

He moved close to her. "Jamie loves you and misses you."

She shook her head, confused. "How do you know that?"

His mouth twisted at the corners. "Because we all love you and miss you."

"Oh." What? Maybe she wasn't hearing words right any longer. She didn't really get it. What was he saying?

"Where's my bill?" he asked.

"Don't worry about it." She waved a hand in the air. "I'll take care of it."

"Okay." He smiled. "Then I'll just leave you a tip."

He put a small box on the counter. She stared at it.

"It's not a snake," he told her. "Go ahead. Open it."

She turned to look at him, terrified. "Max, what is it?"

"Open it and find out."

Her heart was beating so hard she could hardly make out what he was saying. "I don't think I should."

"Come on, Cari. I dare you. Do it."

Her fingers were trembling so hard she could hardly hold the box, but she managed to open it. Inside, set against black velvet, was the most beautiful diamond engagement ring she'd ever seen.

"Max!"

She turned to find him on one knee.

"Cari Christensen, I love you with all my heart," he announced to her and to everyone else in the place. "I need you in my life. Jamie needs you, too. He's got a grandmother, but he needs a mom. So here's the deal. Will you marry us?"

"Oh, Max, get up off the floor."

"Not until you answer me."

"Of course I'll marry you," she said, pulling at his hand and laughing at the same time. "I can't believe it took you so long to get over here and ask me."

EPILOGUE

THEY started out planning a small, simple wedding, but naturally, that didn't last. In no time at all, it grew into something monstrous. So it was a good thing they knew a good caterer.

They decided to have the event out on the ranch. Cari wasn't so sure at first, but once she saw the changes Max was already making, she was convinced. The driveway was lined with newly planted trees. The main farmhouse was still being renovated, but the lower floor was usable and a couple of the outer buildings, including the bunkhouse, were looking sturdy with new repairs to their structures and a couple of coats of new paint that left them gleaming. The sweeping area that made up the yard was green with new sod, creating a lawn where there hadn't been one for decades. Tables were set up on it, and a radius of white chairs for the ceremony. White tablecloths and silver vases filled with tulips decorated each table. The scene was magical.

People from all around the area began streaming in

an hour early. The ceremony itself was short, but touching. Handkerchiefs were liberally in use all around. And then came the reception.

Max and Cari stood in a seemingly never-ending receiving line, greeting old friends and meeting new ones. Jamie was with them when he was awake, and everyone oohed and aahed over him, which was just what he deserved. He'd grown ever closer to Cari, and she to him. As far as she was concerned, he was her baby, and that was all there was to it.

Her dress was a simple, strapless gown embedded with seed pearls. Her hair was piled high and the diamond necklace adorned her neck.

"You're a gorgeous bride," most people who passed told her. She knew it was traditional to say exactly that, but something in the eyes of the people saying it was beginning to convince her it might be true.

The food was spectacular—at least, that's what everyone told Cari, though she didn't have time to try any for herself.

"Does it occur to you," she noted to C.J., who was responsible for most of it, "that you've found a new golden goose with your catering business, one that you are raising and nurturing yourself?"

"That's right, go ahead and rub it in," C.J. snapped. "You won. I lost." But she smiled to soften her words and added, "I can take it. I've been kicked in the teeth a lot over the years. I must say, this is better. It's nice to have a man who adores me."

Cari nodded, watching Randy checking on the wedding cake. "He does do that."

"Yeah. But then, you've got that, too, don't you?"

Cari had to agree. She smiled at Max. He was making faces and gesturing and trying to convey something to her, but she couldn't understand what he was trying to say. She looked at him questioningly, but his mother came up to say something to him, and he looked away, just as Mara appeared before her.

"Hey," she said, beaming at her friend.

"Do you realize you would never have met Max if it wasn't for me?" Mara demanded. "I think I deserve some recognition. A plaque would be nice." She grinned at Cari.

"So you have to admit it has all worked out for the best," Cari responded.

Mara nodded. "Although I'd rather have you in the family than that C.J.," she told her with a sigh.

"Oh, C.J.'s okay. And she sure can cook."

"My, yes. I would never dispute that."

Cari turned away. One of the neighborhood girls who had been hired to help serve was tugging on her satin dress.

"Excuse me, Mrs. Angeli," she said.

Cari thrilled to hearing her new name for the first time. "Yes?"

"There's something wrong in the bunkhouse. Something broke. I was asked to get you to come right away."

"Oh, dear."

The bunkhouse was where they were storing most of the supplies. She looked at the receiving line and couldn't find Max. Whatever it was, she would have to handle it on her own and she'd better do it quickly. Gathering her skirt, she dashed across the sod to the bunkhouse and hurried inside. As she did so, the door closed behind her, the lock snapped, and she was suddenly engulfed in gloom.

"What is it?" She turned quickly and found herself being dragged into the arms of her new husband. "Max!"

"I couldn't wait any longer," he told her, raining kisses on her upturned face. "You are the most beautiful bride I've ever seen. Ripe for ravishing, I'd say."

"Would you say that?" She laughed low in her throat as he began a slow, sexy seduction. "A quick ravishment sounds pretty good to me, too."

She kissed him back, then sighed. "But we really can't. We've got to cut the cake and lead the dance and…"

He said something in Italian and began to peel her dress away. Sighing, she gave in. The cake and the dance would have to wait. Right now, love had the right of way.

CELEBRATE
60 YEARS
OF PURE READING PLEASURE
WITH HARLEQUIN®!

**We'll be spotlighting a different series
every month throughout 2009
to celebrate our 60th anniversary.**

Look for Harlequin® Blaze™ in March!

0-60

*After all, a lot can happen in 60 years,
or 60 minutes...or 60 seconds!*

Find out what's going down in Blaze's
heart-stopping new miniseries *0-60!*
Getting from "Hello" to "How was it?"
can happen fast....

Look for the brand-new 0-60 miniseries in March 2009!

www.eHarlequin.com

HBRIDE09

HARLEQUIN® *Romance*®

This February the Harlequin® Romance series
will feature six Diamond Brides stories featuring
diamond proposals and gorgeous grooms.

Share your dream wedding proposal and you could WIN!

The most romantic entry will win a diamond
necklace and will inspire a proposal in one of
our upcoming Diamond Grooms books in 2010.

In 100 words or less, tell us the most romantic
way that you dream of being proposed to.

For more information, and to enter
the Diamond Brides Proposal contest, please visit
www.DiamondBridesProposal.com

Or mail your entry to us at:

IN THE U.S.: 3010 Walden Ave., P.O. Box 9069, Buffalo, NY 14269-9069
IN CANADA: 225 Duncan Mill Road, Don Mills, ON M3B 3K9

Return to Virgin River with a breathtaking
new trilogy from award-winning author

ROBYN CARR

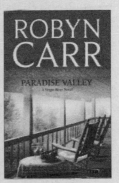

February 2009　　　March 2009　　　April 2009

"The Virgin River books are so compelling—
I connected instantly with the characters
and just wanted more and more and more."
—#1 *New York Times* bestselling author
Debbie Macomber

MIRA®

www.MIRABooks.com　　　MRCTRI09

REQUEST YOUR FREE BOOKS!

2 FREE NOVELS PLUS 2
FREE GIFTS!

HARLEQUIN ROMANCE®

From the Heart, For the Heart

YES! Please send me 2 FREE Harlequin Romance® novels and my 2 FREE gifts (gifts are worth about $10). After receiving them, if I don't wish to receive any more books, I can return the shipping statement marked "cancel". If I don't cancel, I will receive 4 brand-new novels every month and be billed just $3.32 per book in the U.S. or $3.80 per book in Canada, plus 25¢ shipping and handling per book and applicable taxes, if any*. That's a savings of over 15% off the cover price! I understand that accepting the 2 free books and gifts places me under no obligation to buy anything. I can always return a shipment and cancel at any time. Even if I never buy another book, the two free books and gifts are mine to keep forever.

114 HDN ERQW   314 HDN ERQ9

Name	(PLEASE PRINT)	
Address		Apt. #
City	State/Prov.	Zip/Postal Code

Signature (if under 18, a parent or guardian must sign)

Mail to the **Harlequin Reader Service:**
IN U.S.A.: P.O. Box 1867, Buffalo, NY 14240-1867
IN CANADA: P.O. Box 609, Fort Erie, Ontario L2A 5X3

Not valid to current subscribers of Harlequin Romance books.

Want to try two free books from another line?
Call 1-800-873-8635 or visit www.morefreebooks.com.

* Terms and prices subject to change without notice. N.Y. residents add applicable sales tax. Canadian residents will be charged applicable provincial taxes and GST. Offer not valid in Quebec. This offer is limited to one order per household. All orders subject to approval. Credit or debit balances in a customer's account(s) may be offset by any other outstanding balance owed by or to the customer. Please allow 4 to 6 weeks for delivery. Offer available while quantities last.

Your Privacy: Harlequin Books is committed to protecting your privacy. Our Privacy Policy is available online at www.eHarlequin.com or upon request from the Reader Service. From time to time we make our lists of customers available to reputable third parties who may have a product or service of interest to you. If you would prefer we not share your name and address, please check here. ☐

HR08R

You're invited to join our Tell Harlequin Reader Panel!

By joining our new reader panel you will:

- Receive Harlequin® books—they are FREE and yours to keep with no obligation to purchase anything!
- Participate in fun online surveys
- Exchange opinions and ideas with women just like you
- Have a say in our new book ideas and help us publish the best in women's fiction

In addition, you will have a chance to win great prizes and receive special gifts! See Web site for details. Some conditions apply. Space is limited.

To join, visit us at
www.TellHarlequin.com.

Coming Next Month

Available March 10, 2009

Spring is here and romance is in the air this month as Harlequin Romance® takes you on a whirlwind journey to meet gorgeous grooms!

#4081 BRADY: THE REBEL RANCHER Patricia Thayer
Second in the **Texas Brotherhood** duet. Injured pilot Brady falls for the lovely Lindsey Stafford, but she has secrets that could destroy him. Now Brady must fight again, this time for love....

#4082 ITALIAN GROOM, PRINCESS BRIDE Rebecca Winters
We visit the **Royal House of Savoy** as Princess Regina's arranged wedding day approaches. Royal gardener Dizo has one chance to risk all—and claim his princess bride!

#4083 FALLING FOR HER CONVENIENT HUSBAND Jessica Steele
Successful lawyer Phelix isn't the same shy teenager Nathan conveniently wed eight years ago. He hasn't seen her since, and her transformation hasn't escaped the English tycoon's notice....

#4084 CINDERELLA'S WEDDING WISH Jessica Hart
In Her Shoes...
Celebrity playboy Rafe is *not* Miranda's idea of Prince Charming. But when she's hired as his assistant, Miranda is shocked to learn that Rafe has hidden depths.

#4085 HER CATTLEMAN BOSS Barbara Hannay
When Kate inherits half a run-down cattle station, she doesn't expect to have a sexy cattleman boss, Noah, to contend with! As they toil under the hot sun, romance is on the horizon....

#4086 THE ARISTOCRAT AND THE SINGLE MOM Michelle Douglas
Handsome English aristocrat Simon keeps to himself. But, thrown into the middle of single mom Kate's lively family on a trip to Australia, Simon finds his buttoned-up manner slowly undone.

HRCNMBPA0209